The Eye of the Needle

The Eye of the Needle

by B E N   S T O L T Z F U S

NEW YORK · THE VIKING PRESS

First published in 1967 by The Viking Press, Inc.
625 Madison Avenue, New York, N.Y. 10022

Published simultaneously in Canada by
The Macmillan Company of Canada Limited

Library of Congress catalog card number: 67-11265
Printed in U.S.A. by The Colonial Press Inc., Clinton, Mass.

TO DOBRIN

It is easier for a camel to go through the eye of a needle, than for a sinner to enter into the kingdom of God.

Too long now has the earth been an insane asylum! . . .

—NIETZSCHE

the thread . . .

. . . things seem clearer now . . . at least I know with whom I am talking and God is not the terror I had imagined after all. He comes to see me once a week and we talk about different things. I wish I could remember what we talk about but I can't seem to. Maybe if I tried writing them down in this notebook . . . It is a nice notebook and it is mine. Not many things are mine but this notebook and this black crayon are. I wish they had given me a pencil but God said I would be happier with a crayon. God knows best but I really could write faster with a pencil. But what shall I write about? . . . Nothing much happens here. There are the four walls of my room, the bed, the table I am writing on, and the chair I am sitting on. There is also the window and through it the black bare branches of the trees. It is not snowing today but I can tell it is cold outside because there are frost crystals on the inside of the windowpane. The patterns on our kitchen window were just like these. . . . I remember now. I was talking to God about the boy who died. But that's past and besides there's no point in bringing him back now. He's dead. Forget him. It only makes me sad to think about him. Still, God said it might help me to think about him and God knows best. But I really wonder if writing about the boy will help . . . help what . . . I'm content enough as it is but God keeps telling me I should talk to the other people. But I would much rather sit in the garden. Of course it's cold now, so I can't, but I can sit by the window and watch the children sledding on the hill. . . . The boy used to like the snow. Particularly the long tunnels in the deep drifts. He'd dig a hole and call it his igloo and pretend that the shadows of trees and branches playing on the sides of the hard packed walls of ice and snow were as real as the trees outside. The shadows were his trees and he was a bear nestling in his den for a long winter's nap. But what is the use. These are irrelevant details and besides God knows all this anyway. So what is the use of telling Him.

today

God was here again today and I showed Him what I had written. He was very pleased and said I should write something every day. He asked me if I remembered how the boy had died and I said I didn't. But He seemed to think I should. That made me angry. How would I know! Anyway, He said the boy's story sounded interesting to Him and wouldn't I try to write down as much as I could. I said, if I was going to write every day maybe I should have a calendar; at which God smiled and seemed very very happy. I didn't realize it was so easy to please Him. I always thought pleasing God was hard work. But all I said was that I wanted to know what day it was and He immediately sent someone to get this calendar. He pointed to the day of the week and said that it was January. So today is January 7th and yesterday was the 6th and tomorrow will be the 8th . . . But I must have been here much longer. I wonder how long I have been here . . . But it's all the same. One day is as good as another.

today again

I couldn't write yesterday. I was too excited with my new calendar. It's as though time had stopped and now suddenly it has begun ticking again. But what am I doing here . . . If I could only get on that airplane and fly off somewhere. Away from these funny people who sit in the corner and wave their arms in the air. And then there is the cross and Cherny. I don't like the way he holds that piece of wood. It's bad. Like the airplane on the calendar. I don't know why. It just is. No. The airplane isn't. Not like the other one. I can get in this one. That is I wouldn't mind getting in this one if I could only fly away from Cherny. Maybe I can hide it from him. I could cover it with my coat and then throw it in the river when I go out walking. I wonder what God would think of that. He shouldn't let Cherny have the cross. It's a dirty piece of wood. . . . I must remember to ask God to take it away.

today the 13th

Well He wouldn't. I asked God to take the cross away but He said it was not His to take. . . . But it is! . . .

sunday

I did it! I got rid of that stupid cross! Now Cherny won't poison our lives with that any more. But this splinter in my finger is beginning to hurt. Dumb piece of wood. I'll have to go to the nurse and ask her to take it out. But what if she asks me how I got the splinter. I'll say from the bench. That's what I'll say. Nobody will have to know. It's really beginning to hurt though. Particularly with the crayon. It's an awkward thing to hold when it's so short. I must remember to ask for a new one. I wish I had a pencil.

:: 5

January 20

Well, God knew I'd taken the cross and He wasn't very happy. Now Cherny has a new one even though I told God it was dirty. He wanted to know why and I told him it just was. All crosses are. I don't know why. I get angry every time I see one. I'm glad this airplane doesn't have a cross on its side. I told God that the boy didn't like crosses either. Anyway it was the airplane with the cross on it that killed him.

January 21

I had a funny dream last night. I dreamt the boy had come back. That he wasn't really dead. That he wanted to talk to me. But I don't know if I should tell God about the dream. The boy warned me about Him. Said He was not to be trusted. He said God put him in a hole and then wouldn't let him out. That each time he tried to crawl out God would push him back in and he would fall back on the sharp tip of a cross. And it would go through him and he couldn't move because it hurt. And then they would take him off the cross and pour burning oil in the hole in his stomach. And then God would laugh and nod with his goatee. But God doesn't have a goatee. The boy is wrong. Anyway, he said he didn't want this to happen to me. No worry. God and I are friends. I must tell Him we are friends.

Thursday

God was here again yesterday and He said that we were indeed friends. He said the boy was sick and that maybe everything he told me wasn't so. Anyway, the boy's God and my God don't seem to be the same. That's funny. I always thought there was only one God. Maybe the boy is wrong. But he did talk to me and he said it was all God's fault. The big hole, the airplane, and all that. Well I don't know . . . God wants me to keep telling him about the boy but I don't want to. Anyway why should He ask me. He knows all about it Himself.

Friday

I suppose I'll have to write down last night's dream as well, although it's not very different from the first. The boy keeps telling me about being stuck in the hole with the hairs all around the edge and how God keeps pushing his head down under with a cross. But I can't understand why the boy keeps telling me to watch out. The only cross around here, except the one in the chapel, is Cherny's. I wouldn't be caught dead in the chapel, so that leaves Cherny. I can take care of him. . . . I wonder if God would get angry if I took it a second time . . . and there aren't any stinking holes around here except maybe in the women's ward so I can't see that I have too much to worry about there and besides God keeps telling me He wants to help me.

February 1

I don't know why He left me this picture. I don't know the people in it though it does look like a nice beach. It would be fun to go swimming. But I don't see what that has to do with me. I haven't been swimming in a long time. Or

:: 7

have I . . . it doesn't matter . . . besides I wouldn't know. There's only one beach in the summer time where a fast ride down the hills with the two wheels skidding on the sand and the spokes glistening in the sun while you run toward the surge and plunge in through the waves until the first shiver of cold has passed and you are swimming in deep water beyond the surf swimming back now sprawling exhausted on the white sand and the sun baking the sand and the salt on your chest into an earthen brown so that you are the color of the hills and then the long ride back with the sea-salt caked to your lips until you can't stand the thirst except that you know that there will be an earthen jar of ice-cold water waiting for you when you get back and that keeps you pedaling around the curves and you think of how easy it will be riding them down tomorrow and you are glad for the sun and the salt and the water and the green shade of the trees . . . But I can't write all of that down. It would take too long. Besides how do you write something you see . . . I'll just tell God that I don't recognize the boys in the picture. Besides this isn't the beach I knew. Maybe He'll let me keep it though. It would be nice to look at. Almost like looking at my beach.

Saturday

They want me to go to the dance tonight. But I don't want to . . . There are too many holes . . . Besides the boy warned me about them. It's their hair. You dance with them and their hair gets in your nose and mouth and it's like choking. I don't blame the boy for feeling the way he does. I wonder if he's going. I doubt it, but you never know. People are funny that way. I mean unpredictable. Like the boy's tutor. Who would have thought she would stick her hand down his pants. I mean way down. The boy told me all about it. I mean her. The way he started going to her apartment and then the day she wanted to tuck his shirt in and the way she put her arms around him and loosened his belt and how her fingers went way down . . . The boy was pretty upset. He went home and took a bath and rubbed with soap and told his parents he didn't want to tutor any more and his parents said nonsense and he said he didn't want to any more and they said that he was hardly old enough to know what he wanted and he said he wasn't going back and they said he was and so it went . . . The next time she smiled at him and the lesson went as usual and he finished all the lessons and nothing else happened and his parents were happy and that's when it all started. At least so the boy says. But he keeps telling me in pictures and I can't follow him all the time. I'm going to have to put the pictures together. But I can't now. Anyway, I wouldn't know how. God would know.

Wednesday

I told God why I didn't go to the dance and He asked me if I wanted to tell Him more and I said there wasn't any more to tell: that women were black, that they had holes, and that dancing with them made me choke . . . God was a pretty good guy and He asked me then why I thought they were black and I said you know black like crows and He said crows were pretty bad birds and I said yeah and we both laughed and it made me feel good and then He asked me to think of all the things like crows I didn't like and I had to stop and think for a while . . . I said Cherny's cross and some airplanes. But not all. That I liked the one on the calendar. That was a nice plane. But others made me sick. And holes, yes, and black in general, and sometimes yellow, but not always, and that was about all I could think of . . . that I liked beaches but that mountains made me dizzy and He said that was a good beginning and if I thought of anything more to write it down. But that's all I can think of. Anyway, God seemed to feel mountains were pretty bad too, so that made me happy.

February 25

Sometimes I get going in this notebook and I write regularly, while other days I just can't seem to get started. I asked God if He wanted to see it and He said it was my notebook and no one else's and I should write in it whatever I wanted. That I could tell Him anything but that it was my notebook . . . maybe that's why I couldn't write . . . anyway it seems easier now. Or maybe it was that picture of the airplane He brought. Or those pictures. No. It was the plane with the cross on it. The others with the circles and the stars were O.K. But there was something about the stars too. The circles I liked best. But now that I think of it I don't like any of them. I don't know what it was. I wish God hadn't shown them to me. They made me feel funny inside. It was as though the heat had gone off. I was cold and my mouth was dry. Funny that I should remember how I had to go to the john all of a sudden. With that ugly plane. And the next thing I can remember I was all wet and they were picking me up off the floor and my head was hurting . . . this cut above my eye is better but I can still feel the edges where they sewed them together. And this other scar . . . How did I ever get that?

February 27

The boy and I had a good talk. It's funny how he comes in through the door. The others knock but he just comes right on in and sits down on the bed and looks at me with his big eyes. I can't figure it out yet. First he was dead. And now I keep seeing him again. But what is he doing here . . . maybe God asked him to come back. I can't quite figure it out. He told me about the airplane and the beach and the school and the teacher and more about her and all the rest. Funny that he should try to tell me all these things now. I can't see what difference it makes. But then maybe God can figure it out. He's the one who wanted me to tell Him about the boy. But there's something I don't like. Ever since we started talking about him he keeps coming back. Now I know they have tricked me because I thought for sure the boy was dead. And now I'm not so sure . . . Is he or isn't he? . . . Sometimes I think he is and sometimes I don't. Like now for instance. I could swear it was that day on the beach. But when he sits on the bed telling me about it, I'm not so sure. That's the trouble about too many things. You can't be sure any more. I used to know what was what. God was God and there wasn't any boy telling me his God was different. I had my four walls, my bed, my chair, my table, and my window, and that was that. Things you could touch and feel . . . I don't know how I started thinking about the boy and then, well, things aren't so simple any more. What did I care about Cherny's cross, or the airplane, or even the holes . . . things are no longer right . . . Like trying to stand in the rough surf. Every time you think you have a firm footing another big wave comes along and pushes you under. Anyway the problem is trying to put all the pieces together . . . How do they fit? . . . I keep trying to arrange them this way and that but they don't make sense. They keep moving too fast. And the boy doesn't help either. He keeps talking to me in pictures. What am I supposed to do with his pictures. Like the airplane God brought in. What does everybody want with pictures?

March 2

I forgot to tell God about the magpies and the yellow-jackets. Just the sight of them makes my skin crawl. If one stung me again I think I'd go mad. Really. They are evil creatures. The way they move. I can't explain it. But I'd sooner die than have one fly near me.

Friday

It's been a long winter but at last the snow is melting. The ice in the river is going and the sky has that blue purity which only a new spring can give. No sign of leaves yet but I examined a small tree and there were buds ready to grow!

Monday

The problem is to put some kind of order in the boy's pictures. But where to begin . . . I have the feeling I

could begin anywhere. But I'm sure there's a real beginning somewhere. A really real beginning. The thing to do
maybe is to write the pictures just as the boy gives them to
me. That way I can leave the order up to him. Also I
wouldn't have to worry about which came first. Maybe I
should try that sequence about Easter morning. That's a
good place to start. At least I know what he's talking about.
But I don't know whether to imagine them first and then
write. Or imagine them as I am writing . . . I don't know
. . . What would God do? . . . But then He knows it all
anyway! Why doesn't He come out and tell me? Instead of
making me do all the work . . . Why do I have to do anything? I like talking to God though. What will I talk to
Him about, if not the boy. The only thing He's interested
in. Maybe I shouldn't complain. At least not as long as
they both keep visiting me. But nobody speaks the same
language around here. I guess God understands them all
right. But I sure can't talk with the holy boys. Maybe if I
held my arms above my head they would understand. But
I can't. I can't hold my arms above my head all day the
way they do. . . . Impossible. Maybe it's a matter of prac-
tice . . . No . . . At least they don't make me angry.
Not like Cherny.

Tuesday

I didn't get very far. Here I was going to try to put down
the boy's pictures and I never even got started. Good thing
he came again to remind me. Maybe I should just listen to
him . . . write down what he says. Like that bit about
Easter or the summer at the shore with Mara or about the
night the summer moon rippled the surface of the water

and splashed the surf over the sand. The wet sand that still feels cool between the toes. And the clasped fingers holding on to the ebb-and-flow of the waves. Holding on to the sound of the waves which rise to meet the breeze rustling out of the hills. Mara's face is as pure as the moon and we are two white birds winging the night, uplifted into the one-ness of the moon's orbit.

But now the sun's reflection on the water hurts my eyes. The sun has baked the sea to a hot metallic surface that boils the beach and the soles of the feet—the hurting layers of sand burn the skin—blister the shore walking hand in hand with you and the breaking silence of the waves—the silence of our fingertips—the pressure of the sun on our backs, the roaring of the sun at the back of my head, the blinding, burning circle of fire roaring down from the sky—roaring invisibly in the red angry circle—roaring and run-ning and stumbling alone away from the hot roaring burn-ing hurt of the soul and the sun flaming ever closer now mingling with the salty choking cry of the throat, clutching the granules of sand, and spitting the salty, burning black-ness . . .

March 10

Well at least I got this first part down. It doesn't sound like me but then I'm not the boy. And I don't understand all that part about the angry roaring sun. Where did that come from? It doesn't belong. And the blackness. Oh well . . . Maybe I should just sit back and imagine it just as the boy tells it to me. I wish I hadn't started this thing. But I have a calendar now. For whatever that's worth. I do get the feeling that time is moving again. Like the airplane. Except that the airplane isn't really. Not like the one with the cross. I mean—here I am sitting down and the airplane is moving—moving fast. But I'm not. The airplane is moving and I am standing still. Or am I running. No I can't be running. I'm sitting down and the airplane is moving and somehow time isn't the same. Or the place. What are calendars for anyway? . . . That's a nice sun coming in through the window. . . . The first fly . . . Things will really be moving again. Only I am standing still. Sometimes it's better to stand still. Otherwise you get killed. Like the boy. This notebook is for the birds. . . .

March 11

I guess I got angry yesterday. I really shouldn't have thrown my notebook. Some of the pages got torn. Maybe I should recopy them. We'll see what God says . . . but I still can't get those pictures going. If that airplane would only move instead of hover in the middle of the calendar . . . Maybe if I moved . . . Then when I move the calendar stands still. Can't win! If I had a watch maybe . . . I wonder if the trees know what time it is. Sometimes I wish I were a tree. Then I wouldn't get these awful headaches. All I would have to do is lift my arms to the sun and drink the rain when it comes. Then the seasons would take care of themselves . . . and me. Sometimes I think God takes care of me here and sometimes I'm not so sure. I asked Him to make the headaches go away but He said some things have to be worked out slowly. I sometimes

wonder if He's really God. No, not really. But there are
things I just don't understand.

March 15

I can't write any more. I just can't. I get this notebook
out and I start to put something down and it won't come.
I don't know what it is. I'll have to wait till I see God again.

tuesday

He said I should try once more but it's no good
I know it's no good. There's nowhere to go. It's as though
there were too many pictures. All jumbled together. How
do I know which one to take? Or else it's all black. All I
can do is sit by the window. Or lie on my bed.

thursday

What a relief. I don't have to write any more. I told God
there were too many pictures and I couldn't write fast
enough. That I didn't know which one to take. And He
said take them all. And I said that each time I tried to take
one I sort of froze and then it would all be black. And He
said why didn't I try telling them to Him. And I said sure.
So now He's going to write them for me. And He said to just
let the pictures come as they wanted to. And I said O.K.
So He said He'd be back in a couple of days and we could
start. As soon as He changed some appointments. But why
does He have to change appointments? Isn't God everywhere?

the eye . . .

The needle moves through the weave, stitches the design of white checks on the background of the cloth, continuously appears, disappears, and reappears on the white surface of the handkerchief. The thimble pushes the needle though the fibers of the cloth and, each time it passes through, the thread attached to it blends with the gradually emerging pattern. The thread, one white strand looped through the eye, barely fits in the small opening even though it is obvious that it is of the thinnest imaginable.

She is holding the needle in her left hand now and, with the other, is trying to thread it—holding the needle up on a level with her eye—holding it up to the window so the light will pass through the eye—moistening the strand between her lips and tongue and trying, once again, to insert the tip through the tiny hole. She threads it carefully now, draws the strands together, ties a knot on one end, and pulls it tight with a deft maneuver of her thumb and forefinger.

She is once again sewing a pattern on the white surface of the handkerchief. Not on the whole surface, however, just on one of the edges. To make it look nice. The feminine touch. For a woman's handkerchief.

A ray of sunshine, slanting diagonally toward the rug, is illuminating a few particles of dust. The tiny weightless filaments float aimlessly up and down the beam of light and, each time a particle strays outside, it becomes invisible. The oblique ray seems alive with reflections from the countless small grains of suspended matter. Tiny grains of dust cross and recross the barrier of light (which is no barrier since it stops nothing but merely suggests the outline of the visible). They dance up and down, back and forth, lazy and purposeless, following the slight currents of air circulating in the room.

A sudden turbulence swirls the dust particles, swirls them in and out of the visible ray of light, always bringing new particles to replace those which have apparently disappeared beyond the barrier of the upper diagonal. The lower diagonal is absolutely parallel to the upper one and it is only within this narrow band of light, no wider perhaps than six inches, that the disturbance is noticeable. It is impossible to blow the dust particles out of the light beam and, in spite of the effort, new grains appear, swirl, disappear, and evolve within the now decreasing violence of the movement.

The blizzard has been blowing for two days now. Snow has been swirling over the treetops, over the branches, the bushes, the paths, and the roads. It covers the slopes of the foothills, masks the dried grass and the black earth of the lowlands with white, drifts high banks in the gullies, and covers the farmers' fields with deep grain-protecting layers. The landscape is now entirely white. The only suggestion of black is the presence of a flock of crows sitting motionless in the corner of one field.

A fly has landed on the folds of the handkerchief but her hand scares it off into the diagonal of light. Its wings glint momentarily in the sun before it strikes the window pane where it is now buzzing loudly in the lower right-hand corner. The four panes of glass are held together by two pieces of wood—one vertical and one horizontal—which intersect in the middle of the window. The sky is framed by the wooden crosspieces.

Outside the snow is falling, drifting through the air, covering the fields which are now white, covering the checkered fields being outlined by the clever movements of her fingers and the needle—the sharp tip of the needle—which is sewing the small square outlines of a weave on the larger square of the handkerchief—appears, disappears, and reappears. The trees outlining the farmers' fields lend a vast checkered effect to the snow-covered flatness of the region interrupted, here and there, by the diagonal crossing of a road or the apparently aimless meandering of a small river which loops around itself before it passes under a bridge in the far distance. The thimble is pushing the eye of the needle through the cloth while, on the other side, nimble fingers retrieve the slender shaft of metal, insert the tip and, with an apparently endless continuity, repeat the necessary and sometimes tiring motions for the elaboration of the final pattern.

The needle moves deftly through the cloth, weaves in and out while her wrist and clever fingers manipulate the design that is slowly taking shape in one of the four corners.

"Do you like it?"

"Uhm . . ."

"Never mind. But you could at least admire the delicacy of my work."

"Do I have to?"

"All you have to do is live and die . . . And obey your parents . . . Isn't that why I'm here?"

The ray of sunshine, slanting diagonally through the window, illuminates the particles of dust. The lower diagonal is absolutely parallel to the upper one and it is only within this narrow band of light, no wider perhaps than six inches, that the weightless floating filaments of dust are clearly visible. Tiny grains cross and recross the barrier of light, slowly and aimlessly, following the invisible shifts of air circulating in the room. The sudden turbulence swirls the particles, swirls them in and out of the visible ray of light, always bringing new particles to replace those which have apparently disappeared beyond the barrier of the upper diagonal. It is impossible to blow the grains of dust out of the light beam because new particles appear, swirl, disappear, and evolve within the violence of the illumination.

The sky is visible through the four panes of glass intersected by the two crosspieces. One is vertical and one is horizontal, and they are discernible only as two dark shadowy segments, though there is probably a groove of putty holding the panes together. The putty is in shadow, however, like the rest of the wooden frame which now looks like the outline of a cross etched against the sky.

The boy is opening the window, smelling the cold air and inhaling the fragrance of new snow. Millions of snowflakes are covering the countryside with white—a white that now lies heavy on the needles of fir trees, slopes the valleys, hides the contours of the hills, narrows the stream, and etches the tree trunks in black. The snow has covered animals, people, and houses from whose chimneys the blue smoke of wood fires can now be seen curling straight up into the rapidly freezing night air. The first stars are beginning to shine.

They glisten small and far away in the transparent and

now fading night. The sky over the city is full of the droning of planes. The guns, once again, begin to boom while the searchlights finger the sky, and crisscross nervously into patterned shadows of light and dark. Tracer bullets spring forth, multicolored, and then disappear—hyphenated. The air is now full of the density of patterned sound —of red and white lights moving freely in front of the black sky and the to-and-fro weave of the searchlights. A tracer bullet is moving horizontally and, as the lights shift quickly into position and focus in multiple triangles, the guns thunder so insistently that the red spot explodes and burns like a nova.

The boy opens the window, smells the spring air, inhales the fragrance of the pear tree blossoms, and listens to the wind blowing the white flowering of the branches. The fields are turning green now, a green lit by flaming crocuses. The willows bow their elongated leaves into the river while the wild-plum trees illuminate the countryside. The wind is blowing incandescent petals from field to field—forms eddies of white—swirls miniature snowstorms on a landscape of variegated greens and browns—drifts the petals of new fruit fertilized for the coming season in the aftermath of winter—as though winter would not depart—but it is not winter because the coronae of the trees dot the countryside with an explosion of white.

Spring is blowing through the window—blowing around the ears and nostrils—blowing hair and the roots of hair—caressing the cheeks and the eyes—permeating the very pores of the skin—enveloping the neck and shoulders —stirring, spreading, germinating, uncurling new shoots toward the sun—unfolding, expanding, pulling new life out into the open—spreading it against the sky, favoring the flow of sap, the budding, blossoming, and fertilizing of each species and the growth toward fruition under the hot but benevolent rays of the sun.

The sun is slanting through the open window and, in the distance, it is shining on a yellow sea. The wind moves the ripe heads of wheat, bends them into an evolving mass that is now waving the hot gusts of summer. The sea swells and sways its surface, expands into deep troughs, readies itself for the unfurling of the next wave, and then heaves its ripening presence into long billows. Summer momentarily flies the wings of the meadowlark high above the sound of droning insects.

A yellowjacket is flying over the short green grass of the pasture. It is no doubt buzzing over its hole, or has perhaps even settled on the edge. Its wings are folded above the black and yellow bands of its abdomen, and it hovers nervously while the eyes, mandibles, tentacles, wings, and body of an identical insect emerge from the hole in the ground. The two yellowjackets remain poised for a moment on the narrow circular band of earth then, as others arrive, either from distant fields or out of the opening, some dart into the hole while the emerging ones fly off with a faintly audible buzz.

The sea of wheat next to the pasture is swaying, bending, rolling, and unfurling itself. The waves undulate the surface, move it as far as the edge of the field where they come to rest on the short grass. The boy is stamping the grass with the heel of his shoe, stamping on the hole now, jumping up and down on the small opening in the ground from which more yellowjackets are beginning to emerge. . . . The first sting is on the leg and even as the realization of what is happening sends him running across the pasture, the stings on his neck and ears are like hot painful stabs in the crying sweat of the afternoon.

The insects are burning a hole in the sky—a red angry hole that is now roaring in his ears—burning the back of his head with hot stabs that sound like the chatter of machine guns.

But it is only the rustling of leaves. And in the fall the odor of damp earth wafts through the open window, pumpkins glow in the fields, and apples thump to the ground. On chilly afternoons the geese can be seen flying south, plying the sky in honking triangular formations. The storks no longer wade through the swamps and the swift flight of the swallows has carried them also to warmer lands. There is perhaps the early bite of frost covering the grass with crystals that crunch underfoot and leave dark wet footprints on the lawn. Later in the day the wind will pick bushels of red and yellow leaves and send them rolling pell mell over the fields, splashing the countryside with wisps of color. And when the autumn clouds descend over the mountains and the farmers have plowed their fields, leaving long overturned furrows of black earth, flocks of crows will gather in the wake of the sower, and the days will be raw with the chill of winter cold.

With the first freeze the farmers pray for snow. They pray for its protective layer to safeguard their winter wheat. Some winters, however, the freeze is early and the snow

late and if the cold is too severe the earth cannot protect
the grain in the furrows, even the kernels that have escaped
the black beaks of the crows. During cold snowless winters
the grain dies and, in the early spring, when the shoots
should be knifing their way into the sun, the fields remain
black, there is no green layer of reassurance, and even the
crows spend their days more productively raiding the nests
(so they say) of other birds.

On such days their cawing can be heard from the treetops and their heavy flight, as they lumber over the fields,
blights the countryside and etches their wings against the
sun. They descend raucously into the upper branches of
trees, bend the slender twigs, flap their feathers to maintain a precarious balance, or, unable to do so, drop down
into the tree itself where, presumably, the eggs of the song-
birds lie exposed to the hungry pecks of their beaks. Once
broken and the eggs sucked dry the raiders depart as
raucously as they arrived, flapping their wings, lumbering
over the streams and fields in search (it is said) of new
nests and the small yolks of other eggs. Even the cuckoo,
that other predator who lays eggs and never hatches them
herself, suffers the devastation of what the farmers, not
infrequently, call the black plague. "Yes," they say, "it is
another year of the plague." And they dust off their shot-
guns, patch up the stuffed, motheaten owl, trudge into the
fields, and prop him on a fence post. It is then the crows,
ever sensitive to the presence of their arch-enemy, after
blackening the sky with their cawing and their circling
and their flapping of wings, descend. A well-aimed shot
will bring down two or three at a time and still they hover

and dive at the owl, as though their hate were so strong that they remain oblivious to the danger of the gun which otherwise they sense and keep their distance from. When the ground around the decoy is covered with dead birds, the farmer recovers his weatherbeaten trophy, takes it home, stuffs it away in the attic for the next plague year, and leaves the crows to rot in the sun.

The spot on the rug forms an oblong patch whose brightness contrasts with the darker area around it. An imaginary line separates the edge of the shadow from the brightness itself. The illumination, perhaps a foot long and around six inches wide, forms a kind of parallelepiped in the middle of which a fly is laboriously and assiduously preening its wings. It may be the same fly seen earlier on the handkerchief and heard buzzing in the lower right-hand corner of the window pane. No insect is now visible against any of the four panes of glass and there is no glint of wings in the diagonal ray of sunshine. The band of light no wider, perhaps, than six inches is defined by two imaginary parallel lines within which the grains of dust continue to reflect the sun.

The fly is rubbing its hind legs, intertwines them, separates them, scrapes, rubs the wings now, polishes them with repeated and careful movements, depresses the veined, semi-transparent filaments, scrapes them, re-rubs, disentwines, sets the legs flat alongside the others, and then begins again the entire sequence of minute and detailed motions.

"Have you finished the poem?"

"No. Not yet."

The needle moves rapidly through the white checkered weave. She is holding it in her right hand and the handkerchief in her left. Two strands of white thread are dangling from the eye. The slender thread barely fits through the tiny hole even though it is obvious that the strand is of the thinnest imaginable. The thimble is pushing the needle through the fibers of the cloth, pushing it through the intermeshing threads of the design.

She is sitting crosslegged on the bed, the needlework in her lap, her head and neck bent slightly to the left and, with repeated and nimble movements of her right hand, continues to push and pull the needle in and out of the fabric.

"How many are you going to do?"

"How many checks?"

"No, handkerchiefs."

She smiles, as though to herself, enigmatically, sitting crosslegged on the bed with her head to one side and her black hair hanging loosely in front of the left side of her face. Every so often, she interrupts her work to smooth its mass—to brush it back with an impatient gesture—as though it would intrude on her concentration and alter the sequence of her design. It is a futile movement, however, because, as she bends her head again, the curls fall back in front of her eye, undulate along her cheek, and flow, suspended, over the pattern.

Now she is sitting on the stool in front of the mirror and the smile of her reflection is as enigmatic as the invisible smile which is its source. Her lips part in a gentle pout that, immediately and with incredible mobility, reveals her teeth, not laughing, mocking perhaps, condescending, no, the parting of the lips is too rapid to be certain. There is only the high arch of the eyebrow and the white teeth of the comb locked in the mass of hair.

The teeth flow along the perfumed curls and comb their turbulence. But the static sounds like fire. Electric filaments lick the air, consume themselves in a rapid sequence that ripples the surface of duration, forks, multiplies, evolves, and then flows the heat of its mass through the open door of a furnace.

The wind is blowing her hair, blowing it swiftly back and forth; it ripples the edges, undulates the design, snaps it briskly back and forth—flaps, ripples, and crackles it like fire.

The flames lick the red surface of duration, fork, multiply, evolve their metamorphosis, and then consume themselves in a succession of waving tongues.

She is combing the turbulence, lifting the black emblem, and spreading it against the sky. The teeth are unlocking the tangled filaments and, perhaps, ordering their flow.

The emblem flaps in the wind—flaps, turns, whirls, and revolves—faster and faster—until the violence spreads night across the moon.

Only the morning star is visible, small and far away. A dozen or more people—men, women, and children—no more than silhouettes, are huddled together where they are standing on the hill. They listen to the explosions, watch the bursts of sound and the red glow above the distant cityscape while, in the interim silence, the crowing of a rooster or the barking of a dog remains, lost, somewhere on the dark flat plain that separates the city from the hill.

The people are staring at the illuminations on the horizon. The sky over the city is now full of the droning of airplanes. Searchlights finger the sky and crisscross nervously into patterned shadows of light and black, while tracer bullets spring forth, multicolored and red, and disappear—hyphenated. One tracer bullet burns brightly in the air, the searchlights move quickly into position and focus in multiple triangles on the red spot which is now accelerating. The guns thunder until the spot explodes and burns like a nova. In the ensuing silence the cry of the cocks is heard once more; even the murmur of the river below the hill is audible. The bombers have now passed and the incendiary bombs have ignited red clusters that rise and fall on the horizon.

"Do you think the pilot got out?"

"Ammunition train, I imagine."

"Are they coming back?"

The group of people remains on the hill, remains standing until the morning star burns itself out. Then, silently, by twos and threes, they turn around and walk back through the path in the woods to their homes. The bells of Easter are ringing over the plain.

The sky, visible through the four panes of glass, is intersected by the two wooden crosspieces. The pieces, one vertical and one horizontal, are only discernible as two dark segments though there is probably a groove of putty holding the panes in place. The putty is in shadow, however, like the rest of the wooden frame. The cross is now plainly visible.

The wood has a distinct lengthwise grain. The vertical segment is probably one foot long while the horizontal arm, slightly above center, is much shorter. It is more or less standard, with no specific distinguishing characteristics except that, obviously, it has been hanging for many years on the wall above the blackboard.

A plump rosy-cheeked boy is trying to solve an arithmetic problem. He is wearing very short pants, even though it is a cold early December and Brother Polycarp, in his impatience over the boy's slowness, has taken a slender elongated map pointer with which he is switching the boy's bare legs. Each time the pointer comes in contact with his epidermis it leaves a red mark. The problem in arithmetic is not being solved and the class is now laughing.

There are five red marks on his legs and the pointer is winging through the air for the sixth time. The boy winces but does not rub the back of his thigh. A few tears are nevertheless visible on his cheek. Brother Polycarp sends him back to his seat.

It is, more or less, a standard wooden cross with no specific distinguishing characteristics. The lengthwise grain is more pronounced because of the dust, or perhaps even dirt, which has lodged in the perforations. The wood itself is light, however, and the horizontal arms, which are slightly above center, are shorter than the vertical segment centered in the middle of the wall over the blackboard.

The two white flaps of Brother Polycarp's collar are hanging down flat and starched. A perforation in the center of the collar delineates the two flaps with a thin black line which is not really a line but merely the portion of his robe visible through the perforation. The flaps are square at the ends and starched to a dazzling white which contrasts with the robe and accentuates the parallel lines and perfect symmetry of the squared tips. Brother Polycarp's arms are lying extended on top of the desk while the palms of his hands are firmly clasped. In this position the black sleeves articulate at the elbows and, alternately, move up and down between the goatee and the top of the desk.

"None of us knows how long the occupation is going to last nor how long this particular school will remain open. In the meantime it is your duty, in the eyes of God and man, to continue your education and to use profitably the advantages which are being offered you. Some of you, I know, in the light of recent events, may feel less responsible than before, but, let me assure you, there is a challenge in adversity and, if I may quote Hugo, 'Birds fly more strongly against the wind.' I shall, therefore, continue to expect the usual high standard of work and you who have been lax over the past few weeks can now resume where you left off or, rather, where you stopped working. It would be best, perhaps, in the future, if I did not have to refer to these matters again, for reasons which I think must be obvious to everyone. You are the future generations and it is only fitting that until circumstances actually prevent you from learning you continue to do the thing which will eventually . . ."

The sleeves of the robe are on top of the desk, the hands are clasped, the goatee is moving with the mouth and lips and the contours of each thought—the voice talking and stopping and talking and elaborating the meaning of his intention—while the flaps of the collar, starched to an incredible whiteness and hanging down flatly and with squared-off ends, are outlined against the black surface.

"The war may last for years . . ."

The cars, carts, and wagons are moving along the main road in a long diagonal line that stretches across the fields. The wagons are full of beds, chairs, tables, women and children, while the baggage racks of the cars are heavy with suitcases and the overlapping lengths of mattresses. The cars are following the horse-drawn carts and the people on foot are walking beside them. The line is passing over the bridge but some of the figures leave the road in order to follow a narrow loop-of-a-path that leads to the river beneath the span. It is the same river that meanders aimlessly through the countryside and loops around itself many times.

There is still, perhaps, a dog's carcass lying in the river bed or washed ashore by the high waters, drowned in a sudden torrential cloudburst. It is no doubt a sheep dog—one of a half-dozen that follow the flock and protect it and the shepherd in the daily round of pasturing that takes place on the stubbly grass of the foothills. Or perhaps the dog was killed in a fight. Without its collar of protective spikes it could have succumbed to the snarling fangs of a more aggressive hound. Or it could have been ripped apart by a pack of dogs and its fur scattered to the winds. The young shepherds sometimes sic the dogs on each other in an attempt to alleviate the tedium of following the sheep day after day after day. They will even let the dogs chase a passerby and, on such occasions, if there are no stones to hurl, the yapping beasts come dangerously close, snarling and biting at your ankles.

One leg is dangling over the side of the bed while the other one is tucked under her. The thimble is pushing the needle through the cloth of the white handkerchief while, no doubt, on the other side, nimble fingers retrieve it, then insert the tip in the weave, and pull it through again. The arm extends, the wrist flexes, and the hand returns the needle to the corner of the handkerchief where the pattern of white continues to evolve. The checkered effect of the farmers' fields is interrupted, here and there, by the diagonal crossing of a road and the apparently aimless meandering of the river which loops around itself before it disappears under the bridge. The cars and wagons are moving along the road in a line that stretches as far as the eye can see.

She is dangling a leg over the side of the bed. The ray of sunshine has shifted and is now no longer illuminating the nap of the rug but is shining, instead, on the contours of her calf and shin. The leg, from the articulation of the knee-cap, around the bulge of the calf, and as far as the ankle, is now in sunshine. A few grains of dust are hovering in mid-air, suspended aimlessly, slowly revolving in the infinitesimal and barely perceptible currents of air generated, perhaps, by the warmth of sun passing through the window. The horizontal arm of the wooden segment holding the panes together is casting a shadow which cuts the leg in two. The shadow is passing across the shin bone at a place equidistant from the articulation of the knee and the slight sideward protrusion of the ankle bone. She is now swinging her leg, articulating it from the knee so that the dark band of the shadow moves up and down lengthwise along her leg all the way from the bony indentations of her knee to the slender tapering of the calf at the ankle.

She is flexing her foot, arching her instep which curves from the heel as far as the symmetrical row of toes—the row of toes on which the shaft of sunlight is now shining. The particles of dust are again swirling within the narrow band of light. The storm has been whirling the snowflakes out of the sky, drifting and accumulating them in snowbanks on which the sun is now shining, illuminating the landscape with reflections that pierce the eyes and nostrils with penetrating, almost antiseptic, cold. The heavy contours of the branches and bushes cast bowed shadows on the slopes of white over which, somewhere in the distance, the echoing report of a rifle is heard, followed by the bark of a dog. A hunter's dog, no doubt, for the rabbit tracks seem to go over the hill in the direction of the sound. The tracks are visible as four small round holes. There is a fuzzy outline of claws made by the unevenly spaced indentations of the feet, followed, in turn, by the almost imperceptible scratch of the cottontail. One imagines the rhythmic hopping of a rabbit leaving a continuous succession of footprints that extend infinitely, it seems, over the white surface of the snow.

The footprints follow the tree-line along the top of the hill and enter a clump of bushes. The snow inside the bushes is rolled and matted down where the rabbit either slept or rested. The tracks then emerge on the other side of the clump, follow the hill down to the river which, at this point in its course, loops around itself, and the rabbit, as though seduced by the loop, has followed the snowy banks to another cluster of bushes on the far side. The succession of four little round holes with the outline of tiny rabbit claws and the scratch of the fluffy tail are clearly visible. The footprints of the hunter have left heavy marks in the snow but, rather than follow the rabbit directly into the cluster of bushes, he has skirted the high snowbank and has approached it from below. But there is no rabbit; only a few rust-colored stains, blood no doubt, where the hunter shot the rabbit and the dog barked. There are a few wisps of fur and brown hairs left on the dirtied surface of the snow. A few shiny brown hairs tipped with white are lying flat near the uneven clotted stains. The wisps of fur are lighter in color, from the belly no doubt, and there are more of them, scattered at random, forming no particular pattern, just lying on the surface of the snow where the rabbit crouched with its belly exposed to the blast of the shotgun.

She is not sewing any more. Her toes are moving across the room, back and forth, making invisible tracks on the nap of the white rug. Her ankles and high arch are stepping nimbly, almost running, while in the ray of sun the particles of dust swirl violently from the currents generated by her passage.

There is the sound of running water. The shower must be splashing the white tiles, perhaps also the cluster of black hairs which forms a particular pattern. Her belly is no doubt also exposed to the blast of water. Strange that the wisps of hair under the armpits should be lighter in color while the triangular cluster of hairs forms a black shadow on the otherwise white surface of her skin. In order to see more the eye has to angle itself sharply downward or upward through the narrow aperture of the keyhole. The key is missing, perhaps lost.

But there is no rabbit in the bushes, only a few rust-colored stains, blood perhaps, where a few hairs, tipped with white, are lying flat near the uneven clotted stains. The wisps of fur are lighter in color, scattered at random, forming no particular pattern, just lying on the surface where she is standing with her belly exposed to the blast of the gun.

No, she is lying on the bed, asleep probably, while the sudden, elongated, high-pitched, continuous grating noise of a locust rasps and rasps its dusty and persistent stridence. The angle of the roof casts its shadow on the lawn while the sun illuminates the green grass around it. She is lying on the bed in a chemise which falls loosely over the contours of her body. The chemise moves with the rhythm of her breathing and creases ever so slightly over her breasts. The long gray barrel of the gun is pointing at the insistent shadow between her thighs.

The pieces of wood—one vertical and one horizontal—intersect in the center of the window. They need a fresh coat of paint since the old white layer has cracked and is chipping away in many places from constant exposure to the rain and sun. In any case, the two crosspieces are not only rough to the touch of a finger but fairly warm where the sun has been shining on them.

It is a plain cross, its horizontal arms shorter and slightly above center while the lengthwise grain of the wood is dark with age and the accumulations of dirt. The class recites a Hail Mary and then, in unison, crosses itself and sits down to listen to Brother Polycarp's fifteen-minute lesson. His voice is pleasant and persuasive. "And I say unto you it is easier for a camel to go through the eye of a needle than for a sinner to enter the kingdom of Heaven." The whiteness of the elongated flaps, their symmetry and squared-off ends are centered exactly beneath the tip of his goatee.

"Do you know what Polycarp means?"

"No."

"It means many fish."

"Who told you that?"

There is a tug on the line and the cork in the water bobs down and up. The boy is reeling it in, hand over hand, pulling on the weight that is now rising and breaking the surface with scales that glint in the sunshine. It twitches its tail as the wriggling fins arc over the jetty and splash themselves still on the splintered boards of the dock. The gills are heaving wide now, showing tinges of rose on the inside, and the tail, except for an occasional intermittent flip, remains motionless until it is finally and absolutely still.

"So it means many fish, does it!"

The lengthwise grain of the wood is dark with age, and the accumulations of dirt. The layers of paint have cracked and are chipping away in many places from constant exposure to rain and sun. In any case, the two crosspieces are not only rough to the touch of a finger but quite warm where the sun has been shining on them.

"Yes. Haven't you heard of Saint Polycarp?"

The boys shade their eyes to look at the formation of planes.

"Another attack."

"Yes."

"They look like fish."

The planes disappear but in the distance there is the sound of anti-aircraft fire. The two boys sit silently, their eyes on the corks floating in the pond. Several swallows with spread wings skim the surface, dip their white throats, then climb swiftly, trailing droplets of water. The ripples reach the corks in widening circles.

"Saint Peter was crucified with his feet up and his head down, in order, they say, not to die the way Christ did." On a plain wooden cross with horizontal arms shorter than the vertical segment and slightly below center. The layer of white paint has cracked and is chipping away in several places from exposure to the rain and sun. The crosspiece is rough to the touch of the fingers and almost hot where the sun has been shining on it.

"Polycarp was one of the Apostolic Fathers who wrote epistles and who went to Rome to confer with Anacletus when the controversy about the time of Easter arose between the Eastern and Western Churches. During the persecution under Marcus Aurelius Antoninus he was brought before the Roman proconsul at Smyrna and urged to revile Christ but he refused. The people then wanted to fling him to the wild beasts but, instead, he was sentenced to death by fire. The flames, however, played harmlessly around him. When the judges ordered one of the executioners to run him through with a sword, the flames were extinguished by the blood that flowed from the wound. So they say."

". . . in order to enter the kingdom of Heaven."

The needle is weaving its design of white checks. Each time it passes through the intermeshing fibers of the handkerchief the thread blends with the pattern. The strand

:: 39

barely fits through the eye of the needle even though it is obvious that it is of the thinnest imaginable. In order to see more the eye has to angle itself sharply downward or upward through the narrow aperture. The white square tiles on the wall are clearly visible beyond the specific outline of the hole from which the key is missing.

She is lying on the bed. The creases of the chemise over her breasts stretch imperceptibly with the rhythm of her breathing. Her black hair lies scattered over the white surface of the pillow. A bare arm is flexed loosely on the sheet above her head revealing a lighter tuft in the armpit.

"We are men. You guys are a bunch of boys!" Tony lifts one arm into the air and with the fingers of his left hand pulls at the brown hairs. "Have to fuck a woman before you get hair like this." He steps out of his supporter and slams the door of the locker. "You know how the maid greets me when I get home? Let me tell you . . . with her dress up to here . . . and no panties." He ambles off into the shower room and turns on the water. The sound splashes on the white tiles. The blast from the nozzle is now streaming over the cluster of hairs.

She is sitting in the tub—soaping and lathering and rubbing her hair—lathering it into a thick white mass—rubbing it with her fingertips—rubbing, soaping, lathering, and rinsing. She is pouring water over her head—over the dark strands of hair dripping into the water while trickles of soap are running down the back of her neck—down the wet surface of her rounded shoulders—water—splashing against the sides of the tub—rippling around her knees and the tips of her breasts—the oval rounded shapes of her breasts now visible through the aperture of the keyhole. The sound of the shower has stopped, except for the residual trickle from the nozzle and the final audible gurgle of draining water.

The key, approximately three inches long, is cool and smooth to the touch. It is neither new nor shiny but it still has a faint gloss from the constant buffing against the pants pocket. The keyhole end shows a number of distinct groove marks at the base of the metal perforation where the teeth have been worn down from years of turning the lock. The shank itself is relatively flat in contrast to the section which fits into the hole. Two letters of a word are still visible on the shank: ME. The remaining letters, perhaps four, perhaps five, have been worn smooth. The ME is nevertheless quite clear. The thumb and forefinger fit neatly over the round elliptical portion with which the arm exerts its pressure and transmits the turning motion to the invisible latch. The inside of the elliptical portion has been pressed out in the form of a figure eight and it is the outline of this figure eight which, in turn, resembles the keyhole aperture, less so the eye of a needle. Tony is walking into the line of vision outlined by the figure eight.

"Just a bunch of boys. Eighteen drops, man. Eighteen. That's how many I had last time I put it to her. Anyone here have a pecker like this? Mow you all down. Ack-ack-ack-ack-ack . . . you're dead."

The cars and wagons are moving along the main road that cuts diagonally across the farmers' fields. The long line of people is hurrying away from the city, their assembled possessions piled high on wagons topped by mattresses.

The people carrying large bundles on their heads are walking alongside the cars and the wagons and it is a very long line that stretches as far as the eye can see from the city in the north to where the road curls around the base of the hills to the south. Some of the figures run into the fields— run and fall and stumble and drop their bundles to the side. The line of people disperses. The figures run, stumble, and fall as one low-flying airplane passes over the road.

"Ack-ack-ack. You're dead."

The boy is stamping the grass with the heel of his shoe. He stamps the hole and jumps up and down on the small opening in the ground from which a swarm of yellowjackets is beginning to emerge. The airplane is no longer visible and the distant shapes are now walking back to the road. Some of the forms lying huddled by the road make no effort to get up.

The carcass of a dog lies somewhere, rotting perhaps, on the sun-parched stones of the river bed. The river is reduced to a bare trickle in the summertime but its banks still loop around themselves before passing under the span of the bridge. The forms of the people appear no larger than the pears ripening on the tree. The angle of the roof casts a triangular shadow while the green grass around it seems bright by contrast. The barrel of the gun is pointing at the insistent shadow of the triangle lodged under the surface of her chemise.

"The punishment for dying in a state of mortal sin is hell." The two starched flaps of the collar are hanging down flatly over Brother Polycarp's black robe. The white symmetry of the collar is centered exactly under the chin where the tip of the goatee is flecked with gray. The blackboard has a few random chalk marks on it which the eraser has not dislodged and above it, squarely in the center, is the cross. No, it is squarely in the center of the window pane through which the sun is now shining. Her head is turning on the pillow.

The boy is sitting on the red-tiled roof with his feet braced in the gutter. He is listening to the rumble of thunder which may be the sound of bombs. A crow flies into the branches of the pear tree and settles in the highest branches with a loud raucous caw. It is bending one of the slender twigs while trying to balance its black tail in the wind. He is holding the rifle in one hand while, with the other, he shades his eyes against the sun. The persistent, elongated, high-pitched, continuous grating noise of a locust rasps the dry heat, rasps in the stridence of its own making long after it has stopped and the silence has folded inward on itself and disappeared. The dust from the road has settled in the tree from which the high-pitched sound fills the entire crown and rubs itself into the leaves. The wind sends curling funnels of red dust whirling along the side road in rapidly increasing spirals that dash erratically into the harvested wheat fields where they spend themselves in flying bits of yellow straw. The cars and wagons are still moving along the main road.

Once again the figures are running into the fields and jumping into the ditches. The horses are bucking. Again the sound of distant rumblings, the persistent, itchy noise of the locust, the rustle of wind, the curling funnels of dust, and the long, slow, endless line re-forming along the road. But a few dark shapes are not moving. The light of the sun hurts the eyes.

The glare on the blackboard makes it hard to see if anything is written on it. Nevertheless the grain of the cross is plainly visible above the upper rim of the board. The class is reciting a Hail Mary. ". . . blessed be the fruit of Thy womb . . ." The right arm of each student performs the sign of the cross—hand and fingers moving from forehead to diaphragm and then to alternate sides of the chest. The desks creak as the boys sit down to wait, in an interval of silence, for Brother Polycarp to begin.

"There are two kinds of sin: mortal and venial. Since venial sin . . ." The goatee moves up and down with the inflection of each word. . . . "Whereas it is extremely serious to be caught in a state of mortal sin . . ." The starched flaps of the collar hang down flatly over the black robe. The symmetry and whiteness of the elongated flaps, their parallel lines and squared-off ends accent the thin black line of the robe visible through the perforation in the center. The chalk is also white while the walls are an off-white. The cross above the blackboard is beige, perhaps light brown, striated with dark wavy lines—dust in the grain no doubt. . . . "The punishment for dying in a state of mortal sin is Hell. Lost souls are condemned to burn there forever. To burn and to suffer in incredible agony for the expiation of their sins. Imagine burning your hand on the stove and then multiply the pain a thousandfold. Extend the pain over your entire body and think of its intensity as comparable to the throbbing of the severest toothache. Not a mild toothache, for that is bearable, but in terms of violent suffering—a suffering without end—a suffering which is interminable, relentless, and eternal. Do you know what eternal means? Do you know what it means to be condemned to Hell to burn and to suffer forever without end?"

The cross is centered on the wall above the upper rim of the blackboard. "Imagine the possibility of salvation only if you can lick and dissolve Mount Everest with your tongue. Imagine that, in Hell, you will be released once every million years to go to the top and there, in the presence of the Devil, to take one lick, only one, and then return for another million years of pain, until it is time for the second lick, and then a third and a fourth and so on. For eternity. You realize, do you not, the futility and impossibility of ever reaching the plain below, of ever dissolving the rock of such a mountain with your tongue. Consider then, if you will, in the terms I have just proposed, the hopelessness and agony of spending all of your existence after death in Hell. Is it not preferable then to lead a virtuous life on earth, to follow the Ten Commandments . . ."

The rumbling of bombs in the distance is again audible. The crow stabilizes itself on one of the highest branches of the pear tree—bobs its head back and forth and balances its tail in the wind. Her eyes are closed now and the black curls are spread over the pillow. Her shoulders and breasts are moving imperceptibly with the rhythm of her breathing—a steady even rhythm of the chemise that creases the narrow folds of white cloth. The elongated, high-pitched, continuous grating noise of the locust rasps and rasps its dusty and persistent stridence. The chemise falls loosely over the contours of her breasts and thighs. One leg is bent under the opening of a triangle formed by the flexed knee of the other while between the contours of her thighs are the dark shadowy outlines. The gun is now pointing at the insistent triangle—a triangle in which the bullet is making a round hole. The hole opens to receive the elongated shaft of sunlight that is reaching into the folds. She sighs, straightens out her knee, and the chemise, now, lies loosely over her thighs.

A fast low-flying airplane roars over the house. The crow, scared by the noise, lifts itself from the upper branch of the tree and flies off with a heavy beating of wings. The gun now aims at the body of the airplane. The sights are focused in the center of the big black cross that is outlined in white. The rifle follows the westward flight of the cross, the hand tightens, the trigger moves, and the bullet speeds on its way.

It is making a neat round hole in the center of the cross, at the exact spot where the two arms intersect. A thin vaporous trail of smoke is now streaming away from the tail of the plane. The airplane is banking its wings and the trail of smoke is black and thick. Tongues of fire spurt from the right engine as the plane's bank becomes an uncontrollable dive. Fire and smoke envelop the plane and it explodes into many pieces—a black ball of fire hurtling fragments in all directions—away from the hole in the center . . . No, it is not exploding, there is no smoke—the plane is getting smaller and smaller. It is a dot in the sky, receding fast and very hard to see—a speck so small that it finally and completely disappears in the blue sky.

Breathing at that altitude is very hard. Lungs gasp for air while the cold cuts through flesh like a knife. The boy is on his hands and knees, naked and shivering, watching the wind lift the snow off the high peaks. The storm is attacking his body with sharp particles of ice—whipping the clouds around him—shivering his hands and knees—pulling all warmth from his body. The wind hurts his breathing and fills his lungs with a rarefied emptiness. He opens his mouth, bends his head and neck down, bends his arms with the forward moving of his neck, and tries to lick the frozen surface of the rock. But the tongue sticks to the uneven icy granules and solidifies with pain. The other summits are barely visible where they jut through the clouds high above the world.

No, he is on his hands and knees crawling along the rain gutter. An arm moves back, grabs the barrel of the rifle, and pulls it along with him. He is looking at the woman on the bed, at her closed eyes, and at her black hair spread across the pillow. Her shoulders and breasts are moving imperceptibly with the rhythm of her breathing and the steady even up-and-down rhythm creases the narrow folds of the chemise radiating from the tips of her breasts.

But in order to see more the eye has to angle itself sharply downward or upward through the narrow aperture of the keyhole. The shank of the key feels flat compared to the rounded section of perforated teeth which fit into the hole. The thumb and forefinger fit neatly over the elliptical portion through which the wrist exerts its pressure on the latch. The inside of the elliptical portion has been pressed out so that the ring feels like the letter O. It is much wider than the opening through which the woman is pouring water over her head. The empty shell in the pocket moves freely through the O.

The water streams down over her head and neck, streams through the strands of dark hair and drips into the water in which she is sitting. The tips of her breasts are almost touching the surface of the water as trickles of white foam curl over them toward the darker pigmentation of the nipples. Trickles of soap run down the back of her neck below the black strands of hair, then down the wet surface of her rounded shoulders. The water is splashing against the sides of the tub, rippling around her knees, almost touching the tips of her breasts.

The bullet is making a hole in the center of the triangle. The hole widens to encompass the cross in its circumference while the outlines fade as the brilliance of the circle blinds the eyes. An oblong segment of sunlight reaches across the rug to the side of the bed where the folds of the bedspread are almost touching the floor.

The boy moves along the rain gutter around the side of the dormer window, and climbs up on the tiles. The top of the triangular shadow on the lawn has a head and a body and two arms moving symmetrically up and down. An elongated object is in the right hand, or is it the left arm that is outlined on the grass? The head moves to the left, or is it to the right? There is a shadow on the tip of the triangle and it is moving a head and arms which do not know or care which side is right or left.

Another crow flies into the high branches of the pear tree and settles there with a raucous caw. It bends one of the slender twigs while trying to balance its black tail in the wind. The barrel of the gun is again pointing at the crow so that the sights of the rifle move with the swaying motion of the bird. The hand and finger are squeezing the trigger; there is a sharp report, the kick of the butt on the shoulder, and the image of the crow fluttering through the branches, falling limb over limb to plop on the lawn with a final and faintly audible thud. The crow is lying motionless and black. One feather is drifting down, to and fro, in its interminable, oblique, and wavering descent.

The ground under the tree is covered with pears. They are still falling from time to time, thumping down after sudden hot gusts of wind. Yellowjackets are buzzing over the ripe fruit. Others crawl quickly and nervously over its pocked surfaces. Sharp mandibles nibble through the skin to the juicier meat beneath. The yellowjackets hover, suspended in flight over the round, bulging surface of the pears —hover in a sudden flight of wings and striped abdomen —mouths intent on sucking the nectar of the flesh—as they dart from one pear to the next and crawl their winged bodies and sharp stingers over the sweet fragrance of the now rotting pears.

The yellowjackets are eating their way into the pears. The meat disappears into the mouths and thoraxes banded with yellow and black. The crow is lying in a heap where it has fallen under the tree. The distant figures lying by the side of the road are also motionless. But this time of year there is no water in the ditches. The pears are rotting on the grass and somewhere on a dry river bed there is a dog's head with teeth grinning in the sun. The head on the lawn's triangular shadow is now motionless. But a boy is stamping on the hole.

The key slides into the opening back and forth several times while the letters ME appear and disappear. The shank turns to the right and the latch clicks in place. No, the key is in the pocket in which an index finger feels the perforations of the figure eight.

She is sitting down now and the trickles of soap curl over her breasts toward the darker pigmentation of the nipples. The water of the tub is rippling around her knees, almost touching the tips of her breasts—the oval rounded shapes of her breasts hanging over the water; full and ripe and ripe and overripe are the yellow pears. The fruit is bruised. Mandibles are eating the flesh. Wings and black bands penetrate the holes and whirr relentlessly as the heads emerge. Deeper holes eat their way through the pigmentation but fresh clear water washes the impurities away. She wrings the water out of her hair with a slender forward movement of her fingers, stands up in the tub and wraps a towel around herself, as she tucks one edge of the towel above her left breast.

The top of the dormer window forms a triangular shadow on the lawn where it is bordered by the sunlit surface of the grass. The top of the shadow has a head and a body and two arms. One of the arms is holding an elongated object. The crow is lying under the tree, on the lawn amidst the pears, and somewhere there is a dog's head with teeth grinning in the sun. The head's shadow remains motionless.

"Marc, what are you doing up there? You come down

before you fall off. You hear me? You come on down now!"

The boy slides off the top of the dormer window, carefully moves around the corner.

"Just shooting crows."

"Come on in here before we have to scoop you off the ground with a spoon."

The boy jumps into the room through the open window, pulls the rifle in after him, and leans it against the radiator. She is sitting in front of the mirror combing her hair. The white teeth of the comb are locked in the curls. The black waves swell and then recoil with each movement of her wrist.

"Did you send the letter?" She is eying him through a silken strand, her arm poised in mid-air.

"Yes."

"Yes what. Yes, yes? Or yes, no! How are we going to make a brilliant conquest with your terse laconic indifference? You love her, yes? . . . Then let love speak to her with all the eloquence that ever flowed from the pen and the ardent hand that moves it."

"It's not that kind of love."

The woman in the mirror smiles. Her lips part in an ever so gentle pout that immediately and with incredible mobility reveals her teeth, not laughing teeth but mocking, perhaps condescending, no, the parting of the lips is too rapid to be certain. There is only the arch of the eyebrows. She turns her head toward him, vigorously combing the flowing tide. "I'm sure we can fix that!"

The boy's hand reaches out to touch the black waves but a sharp movement of the comb stops his wrist. "Not today, my good friend." The boy looks at the four small indentations on the back of his hand: four tiny red marks where the teeth of the comb have bitten into the skin. The whiteness of the comb is moving the black mass of hair. The marks on the skin are beginning to fade but the edges where the teeth have made contact are still red. The comb is floating in the sea of hair the teeth still locked in the depths of the stormy waves.

The night wind is rushing through November trees, blowing the moon through the branches that have obscured its passage. "I love you."

"I love you too." Her nose feels cold against his cheek but her lips are soft and so warm is the pressure of her embrace, the blond fragrance of her hair, and the faint flicker of an eyelid, that arms are reluctant to part. "Tomorrow?"

"Yes, tomorrow. But my parents mustn't see me." She breaks away and runs rustling the dry leaves of the garden. The moon is cold and round and clear is the not too distant click of a door. The boy climbs over the wall and jumps down on the other side.

"What time are your parents returning?" The voice is coming from the closet door, muffled now through the folds of the chemise. . . . "I said what time are your parents coming back?" The voice is clearer now, closer, coming closer but still muffled behind the door of the closet and the folds of the slip. "I said . . . no, Marc, no . . . not today . . . Marc . . . no . . ." There is the odor of clothes and the soft feel of skin on the palm of the hands. "Not here, Marc! . . . Not here . . ." The fragrance of a soft pushing, pressing, breathing, reaching magnitude presses her body against the skirts and hanging dresses—into the dark corner beyond the dresses—hands fumbling at the white softness crying to be released—crying and sobbing on the floor—head pressing against her breasts—her arms now closing around his neck—holding him to her—enveloping him with her liquid self and the salty taste trickling into his mouth from the pressure of his closed eyelids—lips moving down, down to the reassurance of her breast—a nipple hardening now under the movement of his mouth and tongue—his body sighing and heaving and sobbing in the darkness of the closet—amidst the scattered high-heeled shoes lying about them on the floor.

"We are men. You guys are just a bunch of boys!" Tony lifts one arm and with the fingers of his left hand pulls at the light brown hairs of the armpit. "How many of you have hair like this?" He smacks George on the back. "The two of us are men. Have to fuck a woman before you get hair like this." He bounces the basketball off his knee. It soars up at the backboard, hits the rim of the basket, but does not go in. "She's a real honey. I'm telling you." He runs forward for a layup and the ball drops neatly through the net. "You know how that wench meets me when school is out? . . . With her dress up to here . . . and no panties. But you guys wouldn't understand. . . . It takes a man for a job like that." He kicks the ball high into the air.

"That will be five demerits for you, Antonio. Don't you know by now you are not to kick the basketball! When am I going to knock some sense into that thick skull of yours?" Tony retrieves the ball and pretends to be penitent. The gym instructor advances toward him with an elongated

stick and begins hitting him over the head. No, the instructor does not have a stick. He tells Tony to go to the shower
room and get dressed. Tony saunters off sticking his tongue
out at the turned back of the gym instructor.

Tony is fighting in the locker room. He puts his head
down, advances toward his assailant, and begins swinging
blindly with both fists. His opponent steps aside and jolts
Tony's head with a right uppercut. Tony lets out a cry,
covers his nose with one hand, and runs out the door.
Fresh drops of blood are shining on the floor. . . . The
drops of blood are no longer wet but dark and dry. There
are no drops of blood, only the light gray cement floor with
scuffs of dirt lying here and there between the aisles of the
locker benches. There is a faded round spot near the door,
perhaps blood, with faint specks of mica imbedded in the
smoothly textured surface.

The boy is on his hands and knees blowing grains of dirt
and dust off the cement floor. He opens his mouth and his
head and neck are bending down now so that his tongue
touches the cold granular surface of the cement. There is
a sound of footsteps and the boy drops a pencil which he
is picking up as the door of the locker room opens. "Hello,
Marc. Thought you'd gone home. We're counting on you
for the game tomorrow." The boy nods his head and the
gym instructor disappears behind a row of lockers.

On the cement by his feet is a small wet spot in the center
of which a darker stain is visible. A few shiny brown hairs
tipped with white are lying flat near the uneven stain. Wisps
of fur, perhaps from the rabbit's belly, are scattered at
random on the surface of the snow. But it is raining now

and the belly is exposed to the blast from the nozzle of the shower. The water is trickling from the tip of matted hairs which are no longer scattered at random. The key slides into the keyhole.

He is on his hands and knees and she is guiding him into the opening between her thighs. He lowers himself onto the softness of her body and waits. He is waiting for her to lift her dress. Tony opens the door, she lifts her skirt and does a pirouette in front of him, her bare white bottom alternating with the black hair in front. The tips of her breasts are almost touching the surface of the water as trickles of foam curl over them toward the darker pigmentation of the nipples, over the rounded shapes of her breasts which he is pressing against his chest. The persistent, elongated, high-pitched, continuous grating sound of a locust rasps in the heat of the afternoon. The boy is lying with the fragrance of her hair in his nostrils, waiting for the orifice between her legs to perform its function, waiting for whatever is going to happen to take place, waiting expectantly for his desire to concentrate into a brilliant yellow.

The woman puts an index finger between her lips, puckers her mouth, and says, "Well, sonny boy, are you about finished?" No, she is lying with her eyes closed, arms outstretched, saying nothing. Roger is lying on the woman. Roger is working away, pumping hard at the callused cunt of a middle-aged whore. The whore puts a finger between her lips and says, "Well, sonny boy, are you about finished?" Roger is working away. He is pumping frantically now, faster and faster until by sheer effort of will and friction the desired result is achieved and he lies there spent, exhausted, angry, and frustrated at the purely mechanical nature of this union. Roger's voice pauses momentarily, he raises the glass of beer to his lips, and takes a long swallow. "I had to pay the bitch too."

The boy is lying with the strong fragrance of hair in his nostrils, waiting for his desire to concentrate into the yellow brilliance of sharp tongues. The filaments are rippling, forking, and multiplying while the tongues are locked in a burning mass. Vigorous penetrations crest on the elongated, high-pitched, grating sound of the locust. It rasps and rasps in the gusts of hot afternoon wind. He is still lying with the fragrance of her hair in his nostrils but the revolving, circular motion of her pelvis has stopped.

She is weaving her design. The needle insinuates itself into the filaments of the fabric and the pattern continues to evolve as the March wind blows through the branches, through the whispering needles of the pine trees, as the south wind blows over the meadows, melts the snow, softens the ice, and trickles the river—continuously and resinously shuffles the needles in a mellifluous sharpening of tips and slender-pronged elongations that catch the wind and scatter a resilient green over the hills—sways the snowdrops, lights yellow crocuses, wings the first swallows over the chimneys, and walks long-legged storks in the marshes—the wind reduces the circumference of the remaining patches of snow—white against the black fields ever so slightly tinged with green—fields of plowed winter wheat germinating slowly in the earth—the wind touches the fragile blades and stretches them toward the sun.

The needle insinuates itself into the filaments of the fabric and the pattern continues to evolve. She is now sewing blue forget-me-nots with tiny yellow eyes and at the moment the yellow thread is passing in and out of the center of the flower. "Remember the first time we made love? I thought you would never begin! You just lay there on top of me. Like a bump on a log."

"I had never made love before."

"But it was interminable! For the longest time I thought you were impotent. What were you thinking about?"

"I was waiting for something to happen. I thought that once inside things sort of took care of themselves."

"You mean just like that. By osmosis or by . . . spontaneous combustion . . . ha, ha . . . Forgive me, I didn't mean to make fun of you. But I have been thinking of that first day. Wondering what was going on in your mind. Wondering how you would react. Why you wouldn't speak to me afterwards. Why you were so morose. Yet at the time you were fine. A little timid perhaps. But I expected that. The way you came to me with red desire in your cheeks. I was even touched by the clumsiness of your actions, the straightforwardness of your need, the insistence of your hunger. And I took you gladly even if it did mean canceling my appointment in town. Because I sensed somehow that you couldn't wait. That there was an immediacy which could not be denied. And then that interminable wait at the beginning and all the time you thinking that is how it is done. Beautiful, my love, just beautiful. But why did you stay away so long afterwards? And why wouldn't you speak to me?"

"It was a bad time. I had a lot of schoolwork."

"Nonsense, my love. You know I would gladly help you with your homework."

"I was afraid my parents would find out."

"But they know you come here when your lessons are particularly difficult."

The ray of sunshine, slanting diagonally through the window, is illuminating the particles of dust. The lower diagonal is absolutely parallel to the upper one and it is only within this narrow band of light, no wider perhaps than six inches, that the weightless floating filaments of dust are clearly visible. The tiny grains cross and recross the barrier of light, moving upward now, following the oblique shaft to the window where the cross is etched against the sky.

It is hard breathing at that altitude. Sharp particles of ice are pressing into his knees and the palms of his hands. His tongue is stuck fast to the cold frozen surface of the rock while, in the distance, the wind is lifting the snow off the high peaks. The wind is sucking the air out of his mouth and lungs and he is gasping for air.

"I was upset because you moved in with us."

"Really? I'm sorry. I didn't realize. I should have been more delicate. Was that it really? It seemed so opportune. As a matter of fact it was your father's idea. Your having to go across town. And in the winter it was late and dark. So when your last tenant left, your father suggested that I take the room. Don't you think that was a good idea?"

"I guess so."

"You guess so! You guess so! All those times you came

scratching on my window, wanting to be let in. All those times you cried on my chest wanting me to do this and that and who knows what all. You guess so!"

"But you started it."

She is tucking his shirt in his pants. Her fingers are loosening his belt in order to put his shirt-tail in. She is standing over him now with her arms around his waist pushing his shirt, smoothing it down into his pants, reaching with her fingers, touching, touching, and he standing, unable to move, as though frozen to one spot and she fingering his hardness and he wondering at the strange, quivering sensation, marveling at the sweetness, feeling the blood pounding in his cheeks, moving now, running fast down the stairs of the apartment building, running hard along the pavement, past the staring faces, along the trolley tracks, through the square, alone, all the way, until he reaches home, still running, up the stairs to the bathroom, breathing hard, scrubbing with soap, scrubbing hard . . .

"Your father told me you didn't want any more lessons but we both decided you couldn't do without help. Wasn't that clever of us? And really now . . . Aren't you glad we continued? Am I not better than some cheap little streetwalker? Because that's where boys like you end up, you know. Oh, I know sometimes you think I am. But that doesn't bother me. I'm not a virgin. But then to look at some of the men around here you'd think I am. Doesn't all that Godliness sometimes depress you? No, I guess it doesn't. But it does me. All the thanksgiving and all the Amens and thank you God for this and thank you God for that.

And two services every Sunday and all the prayer meetings during the week. And the hymns and all the praise. Doesn't it depress you?"

Onward Christian Soldiers . . . rises in unison from the lungs of the congregation as the words of the music swell rhythmically from the pews, blend the voices of men and women, boys and girls, old and young, into a chorus of militant tramping feet, "marching as to war," . . . spreading the gospel of the Saviour, anointing the unfaithful, carrying the sacred word to the less fortunate. The preacher's voice can be heard loud and clear above the others, praying, invoking forgiveness and assistance, in the name of the Lord. He is standing behind the pulpit, tall and resolute in his black ministerial robes, reading from the Bible now, speaking to the assembled people of the angel Gabriel sent from God unto a city of Galilee, named Nazareth: "Hail, *thou that art* highly favoured, the Lord *is* with thee: blessed *art* thou among women . . . for thou hast found favour with God. And behold, thou shalt conceive in thy womb, and bring forth a son."

"Your move, sonny." The boy looks at his father's face, not unkind, inquisitive, demanding, insisting perhaps with a father's impatience that the anticipated move take place; the face he has watched so often on Sunday mornings, the voice he has heard invoking the congregation from the pulpit or reading from the Bible.

There is always the scar, well-healed now, on his shiny round head—the horseshoe-shaped fold of skin—the need to protect the king who is still in check—the white king menaced by the two black bishops and the black queen—

the black bishop hovering in strong diagonal position along the white squares—the other bishop blocking any potential move along the black diagonal squares and the queen, with her fantastic mobility, blocking the only and final anticipated escape. The face of the father is confident, perhaps still slightly impatient, omniscient, demanding, knowledgeable, dark heavy eyebrows slightly raised; the white knight emerges around the angle and blocks the bishop along the white diagonal but the bishop moves in and takes the horse; two lines of alternating black and white squares radiate at right angles away from the white king. "Checkmate." The second white horse is hopelessly distant and the white queen, his protectress, has long fallen, captured by the black bishop.

"John did baptize in the wilderness, and preach the baptism of repentance for the remission of sins. And there went out unto him all the land of Judaea, and they of Jerusalem, and were all baptized of him in the river of Jordan, confessing their sins. And John was clothed with camel's hair, and with a girdle of skin about his loins; and he did eat locusts and wild honey." His father's resonant voice fills the church, reaches the ears of the congregation. His words carry the message of God to the hearts of the penitent, cleansing them of their transgressions, restoring their inner peace, giving them confidence in salvation, healing the weary and the baptized, but only the baptized.

The white pawn in front of the king advances over one black and one white square. A black knight emerges and comes to rest in front of the row of black pawns. A white queen moves diagonally to the last square on the side of the board. The black and white unoccupied squares in the middle of the board alternate with a glossy shine, evenly articulated. Pawns are moving, rooks are advancing, bishops are plotting strategy, knights are jousting even while the queen's power is comprised or enforced, until one of the kings eventually falls, doomed by the forces working toward his destruction.

The white teeth of the comb flow along the perfumed insinuations and lock in the black curls. It is nighttime and she is guiding him into the opening between her thighs. No, it is daylight and white trickles of foam curl over the dark pigmentation of the nipples. Her white bottom alternates with the hair of the inverted triangle and she is doing a pirouette, her skirt forming a circle in the air, like the circle of a street lamp, pirouetting like the alternating flashes of neon lights at the Etoile Cabaret where Roger is now going in to dance with the white and the black queen on a black and white checked floor, drinking out of a bottle on whose label is a little black dog and a little white dog, dancing and barking through the night and into the day during which problems in arithmetic are written and solved on a blackboard with white chalk. Men's collars are white but the robes of the bishops are black. Black is the crow that flies but the airplanes come in the night and in the daytime. Holes are black and blood is black in the light of dusk. There is also the Black Sea and the bats that blacken the sky at sunset.

Night is rushing through the bare branches of November, blowing the moon through the clouds, through the eyes and lips of a tender embrace, through the blond fragrance of her hair.

"My parents mustn't see me."

"Take this letter."

"What shall I do with a letter?"

"Take it and read it. It's for you." Mara is unfolding the small piece of white paper. "No, please, not now. Later, when you get home."

Mara is sitting in a chair holding the piece of paper in her hands. The paper has two vertical creases and three horizontal ones. The creases form twelve square outlines and if one wished one could color the alternate squares black. But the squares are all white and Mara is reading the letter. No, she is not reading the letter. She is afraid her father might see it and take it away from her. She is in the bathroom sitting down and her skirt is hoisted up to her waist. No! no! her skirt is down! She is not in the bathroom! She is not pirouetting! No! There cannot be an alternating white cleavage of cheeks and black pubis! She turns the light out.

There is only the shaft of sunlight coming in through the window. The particles of dust are shifting imperceptibly within the slanting illumination.

The boy is writing the letter. There is a purple spot on his middle finger where the pen has left a stain, a stain which has discolored the base of the fingernail. He takes out his handkerchief, spits on his finger, and rubs the mark with the tip. There is now a soiled spot on the white handkerchief but the purple on the finger is less visible, except for a dark crease along the base of the nail. He is chipping the dried oval stain on the cement floor of the locker room but there still remains a faded rust-colored marking. There is also the darker pigmentation of the skin under the fingertips . . . and elsewhere . . . but there are really three and not four granules of mica imbedded in the cement under the very faded mark. There are a few wisps of fur left on the dirtied surface of the snow. The key teeth reveal distinct groove marks at the base of the worn perforations.

A crow flies into the pear tree. Its black body is balancing in the wind, bending one of the slender branches. The barrel of the gun is pointing at the bird which is now falling through the branches, fluttering over the limbs, down to the lawn where it plops with a final but now inaudible thud. A few trickles of blood mat the crow's broken and ruffled feathers. Several drops have dripped onto the flagstones by the fish pond. But the crow is now in a hole in the ground and, as the tip of the shovel presses it down into the earth, it lets out one final squawk. The black forms lie motionless by the side of the road. This time of year there is no water in the ditches.

The boy is holding the pen in his right hand, waiting for her to dictate the words, the sentences, and the letter. She is pacing up and down the room, stopping in front of the closed window, looking at him, talking, composing the letter he will send to Mara, evoking the sequences he feels incapable of creating; he, writing and rereading what she has dictated during the intervals of silence until the letter is finished and she is asking him at last to reread it and he, beginning with, "Darling Mara," then looking at her, then reading:

Darling Mara,

 I treasure the letters you write me, I press them to my heart and envelop them with the love I feel for you and for the hand that writes them. With each letter I feel as though I am touching you and listening to your voice, your soft and tender voice which I love so much. I imagine you sitting by the window, as I am now, watching the golden leaves and, as I look at the radiance of color, I think of the sunshine of your hair, of the beauty of your smile, and of the exquisite luster of your eyes. And if eyes be the window of the soul, my soul is yours and I would that together they form the everlasting embrace of winged spirits, the intertwining of two hearts, and the pure devotion of our love.

Your adoring Marc

"That should satisfy her, lover boy. . . . No! . . . I wouldn't for a moment think of betraying your secret. I like my role. . . . You may not know it yet but this way I can keep you longer for myself. Besides, I like playing the seductress, mystifier of young ladies; I even like to think of myself as the thorn in the flesh of the godly. Or, rather, you are the thorn in the flesh of the godly, but they don't know it yet. They will some day, however. They will. . . . One day the prick will fester and they will understand the monstrosity of it all. But for the moment you are my little winged bird, my 'colibri' and it pleases me that you should have two flowers from which to draw your honey—the lovely poisonous honey which I distill—do you understand what I am saying? . . . You do? . . . Hm-m-m, so much the better . . . but I wonder. I may be a little faded of course and I certainly don't have the innocence of your little Mara. How old is she now? Fourteen? Like you. Well, I'm more than twice that and by the time you're my age I'll be an old woman but that doesn't matter. It is the now that matters—the fragrance of the now—the sweetness of the now—do you understand—I don't know —sometimes I really think you do but then I wonder— when you cry . . . I wonder. . . . There are things which I don't think you tell me. Though you should, you know. It's not good to lock them up. They fester. Love must be taken on the wing. Whenever and everywhere . . . But then I don't always think you want it that way. Why don't you *not* see me? Go to Mara. I'm only bad for you. I sense that sometimes. Go to Mara and stay with her and love her as you can. No? . . . Well then have it your way. I don't blame you really. Though at your age I may be a wee bit envious. Anyway you have your cake both ways, don't you. Very nice . . . Don't go . . . I'll put the letter in the secret place. Really I will. You don't believe me? . . . So that's my thanks. My recompense for coming to the rescue of the lovelorn . . . no . . . no . . . closer . . . tell me what you see in my eyes. Is it the everlasting embrace of two winged spirits? Is it the pure devotion of your lovely Mara? I know you, sonny boy. You don't want to sully the purity of your little Madonna. But can't you see, by now we all have feet of clay. You can't make love to your little Mara so you come to me. You come to me to write your pure little love letters. If that's what you want, there are some things I want too! . . . No . . . no . . . please . . . On second thought I should, perhaps, not write the letters for you. Let Mara see for herself. And then how long will your hearts intertwine? . . . Sorry. I'm cruel sometimes, I know. . . . I'll play your little game . . . because that's how they want it too. The flesh and the spirit. Only the flesh isn't quite so pure as the spirit. Is it? Well, is it? . . . But at least the flesh is honest. You and I are honest. Not honest with Mara or your parents, but honest between us. You may not tell me everything you think but when you make love to me it's an honest love. You wouldn't agree but there is an honesty in your embrace which you refuse Mara and which your father, God bless his soul, would never understand. Sometimes I think you deceive yourself. But at least between us there is no duplicity. You know what you want and, goodness knows, get, and so do I. In your own silent way, of course. I guess I never expected you to be verbose . . . you know what that means of course . . . but then I wouldn't be writing your letters for you if you were. So I sit here and talk for both of us but that's all right because you know that I am talking for you too. Oh, you don't agree with all of it, I know, but you are aware and you understand what I mean, for myself that is, and you want the honesty of our bodies just as much as I do. Besides, I adore your lithe young body. I really do. No. Don't get up. And giving you your pleasure is one of the loveliest joys I know. Really! And I love every tip of you. From your nose down to here

—to the very roots of your hair I love the touch of you. See, my lips are like the red petals of the rose and I kiss your hummingbird, like this, and with my tongue I will distill the nectars of love. . . ."

The night is rushing through the branches of November, blowing the full moon through the clouds, through the eyes and lips of an embrace, through the blond fragrance of hair and the dry oak leaves rustling tenaciously in the trees. Blowing through the clasped pressure of fingertips and the warm flow of inarticulate love as new as the flight of two white birds; as ethereal, perhaps, as two spirits winging the tips of their glide around the contours of the moon.

"I love you, Mara."

"I love you too, Marc."

"Hail Mary, Mother of God . . . blessed be the fruit of Thy womb" . . . The sharp clapping sound of the wooden-hinged clapper violates dreams and sleep ten times and mingles with the words of the prayer even as the boys stand at attention, curl their toes on the cold hard floor, and blink their eyes at the sudden light of raw bulbs hanging from the ceiling. The boys are reciting the prayer, squinting their eyes at the glare, adjusting their bodies to the abrupt intrusion of daylight. . . . "Amen." There is the rustling of clothes and the scuffing of shoes and slippers on the bare floor as the awakened dormitory begins to wash, brush teeth, comb hair, and dress. It is five o'clock. Boys are washing their hands in the cold water which flows from both faucets and the fingers soon become red and raw and aching and stiff. "Hurry. Hurry! . . . Don't have all day!" It is five-ten. Movements are accelerated in compliance with Polycarp's imperative tone. Unwilling hair is doused with water and combed even as the strands resist, sticking up in the back in spite of deliberate efforts to control them.

Snow is falling in the graying dawn beyond the windows. The boys lined up for inspection are stamping cold feet and blowing on moist, aching fingers. Brother Polycarp, dressed as usual in the black robe and split, white, biblike collar, is scolding the stragglers who are at last passing through the double door and into the dark hallway beyond. Five-fifteen, study hall until six, then breakfast of bread, jam, café-au-lait—study again after breakfast, then a half-hour break of cold air until eight. Classes begin promptly—and there is the daily fifteen-minute invocation after prayers.

Brother Polycarp has also had his breakfast and he is now sitting at his desk inspecting the class from behind the goatee, two rows of teeth, an aquiline nose, and two sharp eyes. He is saying that there is no salvation for a soul in a state of mortal sin. . . . "There is only eternal damnation with the pain and suffering and torment of Hell. Indescribable torment and agony which far surpass anything imaginable on earth. Is it not preferable to lead a virtuous life and, if you have sinned, to confess your transgressions? God will forgive the penitent sinner but woe to him who will not ask for the Lord's mercy because the Lord sees and knows all. He hears our most intimate thoughts and deciphers our most secret intentions. There is no hiding from God because He is omnipresent. If you have sinned, therefore, confess your sins because only by confessing them will you be forgiven. Think of it. The slight penance imposed by the father confessor is nothing compared to the fire of Hell. The fire of Hell is as real as the fire of a candle that burns your hand, but magnified a thousandfold, and so no one, absolutely no one, can afford to die in a state of mortal sin. And I say unto you, if any of you have sinned, confess now, because if you are in a state of mortal sin you are in grave and immediate danger."

A boy is standing on the bank of a swollen and angry river. He is watching the swirling eddies. The body of a dog rises and falls, appears and disappears, emerges and submerges with the rough uneven tossing of the water. No, the head of a boy is visible in the middle of the river. The boy is crying for help. His cries are faint and inaudible, covered by the roar of the angry waves. The boy is being swept downstream and there is no one to hear his cry.

"An accident can happen at any moment, a tile can fall on your head, you can drown, be run over . . . think of it. Is it worth running the risk of 'eternal damnation? Compared to the penance of ten Hail Marys, going without dessert for several days, or wearing a woolen sweater next to your skin."

The boy is standing on the bank, watching the swirling eddies of the fast, mud-colored, cresting river. The drowning head is visible in the middle of the rough-flowing current. People are running toward the river. A man is tying a rope around his waist. He jumps into the water while somebody else holds on to the other end. The drowning boy is crying for help. Voices are urging the swimmer forward as his arms fight the current and the tossing waves. The second man feeds the rope through his fingers. The boy is still crying for help, reaching with his arms, reaching and clasping the head of the swimmer which is also bobbing up and down. The people on the shore are pulling on the rope. The two heads, man and boy, disappear, then appear, and then disappear again while the people on the shore, hand over hand, continue to pull on the rope. They are pulling them out of the water now, congratulating the swimmer, covering them with blankets, talking, congratulating, exulting in the rescue.

"These are joys to be endured for the sake of purification. We should accept them gladly as a manifestation of God's supreme mercy and forgiveness. Because the father confessor has the power to remit your sins in the name of the Lord. Therefore, confess your transgressions and promise to walk in the way of the Lord."

The boy is standing alone on the bank of the angry, swollen, mud-colored river. The body of a dog rises and falls, appears and disappears, emerges and submerges with the rough uneven tossing of the waves. But the rains have stopped and the river bed is dry. The river bed is covered with hot, round, dry stones.

The carcass lies rotting somewhere on the bed of stones. A river of maggots is flowing through the body. The animal seems alive with the movement of new energy. White worms are now the circulatory system. A round stone from the dry river bed drops through a hole in the dog's abdomen and disappears into the bowels. Another stone, smooth and white from spring thaws, bounces off the laughing head. A stick pokes the teeth and several maggots, detaching themselves from the blackened gums, curl on the end. The point penetrates an eye, then a hole in the flank, and stirs the abdomen violently until the stench overflows onto the hot stones. Another stone hits the carcass, then another, and another, sinking into the decay, disappearing into that everflowing movement of maggots, bursting the fragile suncracked skin, riddling the animal with a vehemence that sends spurting blobs of decomposed liquid spilling onto the stones. The smell, the heat, and the flies buzz and buzz.

Yellowjackets are eating their way into the pears. The meat of the pears is disappearing into the mouths and thoraxes banded with yellow and black, yellow and black, and the poisonous stingers at the end. The crow is lying in a black heap where it has fallen. The boy watches the small brass bounce of the cartridge on the tiles of the roof. He closes the chamber of the gun but does not reload. The rumble on the horizon is again audible.

The river of maggots is flowing through the carcass. The smell buzzes with the sting of yellow and black abdomens. But the sound is coming over the trees. The roar of the airplane is fast and near, approaching rapidly, too rapidly perhaps for him to slide down the roof and catch his weight in the gutter. The gutter breaks and he is falling off the roof. No, he is lying in shadow in the relative seclusion of the dormer window. As the plane passes he sits up, lifts the rifle to his shoulder, and aims. The barrel follows the westward flight of the cross.

The river of maggots is flowing through the carcass. It

eats the entrails, ripens the smell of the buzzing sun, bursts the matted hair, and riddles the animal with a force that sends spurting blobs of decomposed liquid spilling onto the bed of stones.

"The length of time a soul spends in Purgatory depends on the magnitude and number of venial sins. The soul must be purified before it enters Heaven. It must be purified by fire."

The flames are dancing over the coals. They lick the air, consume themselves in an endless succession of sharp waving tongues that ripple the red surface of duration and then fork, multiply, evolve, and undulate the metamorphosis of the black burning filaments.

"Of course the suffering in Purgatory doesn't begin to compare with the suffering of those in Hell. The souls in Purgatory are transient souls and they may spend weeks, months, or years there depending on the amount of purification required. The soul of Christ for instance passed through Purgatory like the flight of a bird, whereas it must be obvious to everyone that the robbers crucified with Him, even the one who was pardoned before He died, would have to spend a much longer period of time there before becoming worthy of Heaven."

The robber, lashed tightly to the arms of the cross, is looking at the man between him and the other robber. He has a crown of thorns on his head and on his brow are the trickles of blood. There is an open wound between his ribs and his feet are held together with one large square nailhead. There is an ache in the shoulder muscles where the strands of rope are cutting deeply into his flesh, hurting, pulling, straining, tearing the pain and the cramps of the sinews and the bones and the agony of suspended . . .

Time now flashes wind-heaved clouds, explodes the heavens, cramps the sun, obliterates light, and sends rivers of cold body-piercing wind that will not quench the thirst of cracked lips. "Master, if Thou really be the Lord of Heaven above, I beg and implore Thy forgiveness, for I have sinned." The eyes of the man nailed to the cross are closed. Perhaps he has not heard. "Master, I have sinned. If Thou art the Lord of Heaven, as they say, I beg and implore Thee, erase my sins and forgive my transgressions!" The eyes open, the head lifts slightly, and the lips move. The lips are saying something but the words are drowned in the wind. The wind carries the robber's forgiveness into the heavens where it is rolled around the black clouds with heavy claps of thunder.

The moon slides out and spreads the garden with shadows. Night rushes through the branches of November and blows tenacious rustling oak leaves through blond wisps of hair.

"I love you, Mara."

"I love you too, Marc."

"Babies should be baptized as soon as they are born, because an unbaptized baby soul, no matter how pure in itself, cannot enter Heaven. Not that it goes to Purgatory or to Hell. It is relegated to Limbo where souls do not suffer —suffer, that is, in the sense of experiencing pain—but where they do not enjoy the felicities of Heaven either. Rather it is the absence of total joy which is experienced as a void and hence as an unfulfilled need. And since this is for eternity, you can readily understand the need for ministering to the baby's spiritual needs with all due celerity. Even Christ was baptized in the Jordan River by Saint John."

The boy is standing in the middle of the river. The water is flowing around his knees, forming slight eddies—small circular transparencies moving downstream—caressing the bare legs of the man standing in front of him—of the man dressed in camel skins who is now pouring water over his head—saying something in a language which the boy does not understand but which he presumes to be in the name of the Father, the Son, and of the Holy Spirit. The water feels cool as it runs off the head, down the neck and cheeks, off the nose in a steady narrowing stream from the tip, dripping more slowly now until it finally stops except for one last and final sensation of a drop. Multitudes are assembled on the shore and on the bare hills and, beyond, the warm sun is shining in the sky.

No, the sky is angry and the storm is rolling the clouds in a heavy coagulating violence that hisses red tongues of fire and the bone-breaking heaves of speculation. They hang suspended above the tearing cramps of the rope. With even greater pain the soul's entrails burst into flame; the damned, like tongues torn out by the roots and nailed to metal racks, hang above a fire feeding on the offal of a thousand laughing hyenas.

"If there are any of you who have not yet been baptized you should arrange to have it done as soon as possible. Moreover, baptism itself not only makes entry into Heaven possible but it purifies the soul, washes away all sins, even the mortal ones, and places you in a state of grace. Were you to die immediately after baptism you would pass through Purgatory very quickly and enter Heaven in all its glory."

The goatee articulates each sentence with precision and modulates the contours of each thought. The hands clasp and unclasp, fold and unfold their symmetry on top of the desk, rub the base of the palms, and balance rhythmically on the elbows, up and down between the point of the goatee and the top of the desk. The black sleeves hide the flaps of the white collar while the extended thumbs touch the tip of the gray-flecked beard; the arms move down again and the collar is visible once more—up and down very slowly—fingers clasping and unclasping—Polycarp's voice talking and stopping and talking and elaborating the meaning of his intention, stressing his conviction, caressing the attention of ears, focusing the imagery of the mind on the soul's irrevocable journey up or down the long and difficult road to salvation.

The storm is now pushing the clouds with a violence that tears strips of snow from the jagged peaks and sends them hurtling through the air before they disappear into the abyss. A boy is blowing on cold, red, aching fingers—blowing through the orifice of a mouth without lips, kneeling now on the cutting edges of ice—opening the hole in his face to lick the granular surface of the rock; but there is no tongue—there is only the wail of the wind in the black gaping hole—the tongue and its roots are nailed to the metal rack—while here, above the world, there is only the void—absence—and black frozen joints contracting the negligence of alive and the hard tip of a screaming nipple biting the sun.

Her arms are closing around his neck, holding him to her, enveloping him with her liquid self and the salty after-taste and condensations of sweat. The softness of her breast is hardening at the nipple. He is pressing tightly on the white resistant softness of her stomach and her limbs—the bright hairy insistence of a sharp ejaculating desire—re-volving the orange shadows of the slit orifice—penetrating the depths of the abysmal impossibility—cooling the hot into a blue impotent shrinking, receding, wilting—shorn and fragmented by the wind blowing the orifice of a mouth without lips—kneeling now on the white sheets—casting the sheets aside in black anger—kneeling, kneading, press-ing, squeezing, crying with a frozen absence—falling . . . falling . . . falling . . . into the sponginess of viscous, oozing puddles—pouring backward into a sharp black coagulating pinpoint.

The boy is crawling on his hands and knees. He crawls along the snow tunnel which he has carved in the side of a wind drift, brushes against the sides of the hard-packed walls of snow and ice, digs and tunnels the recesses of a cave, scoops and packs, shovels, pushes, rests, and grunts against the resistant white mass until the hole is large enough and he can rest sitting down. He smells the texture of the snow—bites a few crystalline fragments to assuage his thirst, and studies the outline of shadows against the white sunlight.

He takes off one glove, clenches his fingers loosely into a fist and blows into the hole by the base of the thumb. He then blows on his fingertips and fingernails, blows into the empty glove, and puts it back on. He sits, watching the black outlines of the branches cut across the dazzling surface of the snow beyond the mouth of the cave.

No, he is looking at the dark outline of branches against the dawn, waiting for its light to see the magpies, the long tail and the wings of black and white. He points his rifle into the tangled foliage and waits for the receding brilliance of the morning star. Roosters are beginning to crow and the guns boom once again—boom at the small red spot which shines like a nova and then falls in a cluster of orange sparks. One, two, three, four, five magpies, the sharp report of the rifle, the kick on the shoulder, and the barking of a dog somewhere on the flat plain that separates the city from the hill. The magpies fly off with a rustling of feathers and chattering voices, but one bird drops with a dull thud at the boy's feet and lies there oozing blood from a hole in the chest. The guns boom once more. Searchlights finger the sky and crisscross nervously into patterned shadows.

The outlines of light and dark cut across the mouth of the cave where the wind is now drifting crystals of sand into miniature dunes. The sand sifts through the beach grass, while the wind blows striated waves of sunlight through the blades, bends their shadows over the patterns formed by the grains, and waves the length of the beach with infinite variations that recede into the smoothness of wet and the hasty footprints of birds kicking their spindly legs around, into, and out of the foaming bubbles. The sharp needles of salt water bite the skin while the surf rolls over the eyes and ears—rolls over your head until you reach the smooth water beyond where only the nodding of a white sail breaks the line of the horizon. Then a wave carries you past the breathless arms and your chest crashes the distance held until breathing again, legs on the bottom and the waves that recede while the sun dries the droplets into salt flaked with the rubbing of the towel . . . with the rubbing of the scarf over chapped lips, over the hole without lips, over the hole with teeth, over the clicking menacing orifice of teeth. . . .

She is laughing a prolonged crystalline laugh. She is talking and laughing, coaxing and teasing, caressing the black hair with strokes of the brush—brushing the highlights of her waves, combing the turbulence of perfumed insinuations. The curls swell and recoil with each movement of her wrist. The comb is now floating in the black sea and the white teeth are locked in the depths of the stormy waves.

"Really now—you have been impossible! Morose, but morose, but morose. Surely, there must be some laughter left. Adolescence is a time of turmoil, I know, but for you . . . How can you ask for more? You have your little thing going with Mara. How is she by the way? . . . Oh? . . . Well . . . I see . . . Anyway. When you can't stand the urgency between your legs you come to me. . . . Oh, I don't mind being second choice . . . I know you really love Mara. But how long can it go on? Is that how she wants it too? Well, I'm not complaining because if you slept with her . . . I don't believe it. No, really I don't. No . . . I'll make a bet with you. You sleep with her and then see if you come back to me."

"But you know I can't sleep with her!"

"Why not? Hasn't she got a hole between her legs like everybody else?"

"It's not that."

"But you feel right coming to me. Is that it? Well then . . . Don't think I haven't noticed. I've seen you slapping yourself in the mirror when you thought no one was looking. And I've also seen you hitting your chin with your fist. But why? It can't be much fun hitting yourself. I'll tell you what. Tell me why and I'll write you that letter you've been wanting. O.K.?"

"But there's nothing to tell."

"Well then. Maybe as a compromise you'll let me wear the little cross you have around your neck. But in exchange let me give you something of mine. Let me see . . . I know. This sword broach. This Oriental scimitar with the topaz handle. Genghis Khan. The perfect exchange. Here. Let me pin it under your sweater. The sword: violent possession. That's what we need more of. And this can be our secret pact. The sword and the cross. That's what your father wouldn't understand. Don't you see? He is the cross and I am the sword. And now I have captured the cross and you are the sword. Isn't it all clear? No? Well, maybe the rest can be tomorrow's History lesson. In the meantime you ask your father about the struggle between Rome and Judea. Now for the letter. O.K.?"

Dearest Mara,

Please meet me day after tomorrow under the oak tree in your garden. I can slip out of the house after supper around eight and when you hear the mating call of the cat (I'm good, don't you think?) that means I have arrived. I'm sorry it has

*to be a cat call but it is the only authentic sound I can make.
If your parents heard a whistle I'm sure they would be suspicious.*

*I say I'm sorry about the cat call because you know how
pure our love is. You are my Madonna and I adore you. I
worship the very ground you walk on and I bask in the
radiance of your smile, in the halo of your golden hair. Like
Isolde, you illuminate everything with the sunshine of your
presence. I would scale the highest walls and jump the widest
moats to be with you because you are my love. Every time I
see your eyes it is as though the magic love potion which has
cast roots into my heart sends my bond to you coursing even
more deeply through the sinews of our being.* ·

*I long to envelop you in the purest embrace and I cannot
begin to describe the impatience with which I shall wait for
you in our garden of love.*

Your eternal Marc

The ray of sun is now shining on her hair. Out of its
mass glisten turbulent highlights that fascinate the eye.
The eye plays with the possibilities hidden in the depths,
basks amorously in the liquid coils of watered silk and,
when aroused . . .

She brushes the long strands, brushes the highlights,
electrifies the coils, ripples the edges, undulates the design,
and crackles the filaments. The surface flickers bright
tongues over the mass of coals.

"Did you ask your father?"

"Yes."

"What did he say?"

"He said Judea won."

"Is that all he said?"

"No. He went on for almost an hour. Said it was a very interesting question and all that."

"But what did he say?"

"He said it was at the heart of today's problems."

"Yes?"

"That's all."

"That's all! He talked for an hour and you say 'that's all'!"

"But that's really what he meant."

"Didn't he give you any examples?"

"Yeah. He talked about Greece and Rome conquering the world. And how Alexander was nothing but a gangster, a deified militarist. And Augustus nothing but a deified policeman. And let's see. What else . . . And how the Greco-Roman offensive had brought nothing but war and suffering and how it finally used itself up. You know. Things like that."

"And he stopped there."

"Pretty much."

"But then how could Judea have won?"

"Oh yeah. Well, it seems Judea launched a counteroffensive. But it wasn't military. He said that's how Christianity was born. That people who were tired of war and suffering finally turned to God. That in the second century A.D. the time was ripe for peace and brotherly love."

"And he really said Judea had won?"

"Well. Not entirely. Because there are still wars and things. But he said the fast spread of Christianity throughout the Western world was responsible for the ideal of peace and love which finally forced Constantine to proclaim Christianity as the official religion of the Empire."

"That's very good. Your father is an intelligent man. But that's only one side of the story. Tell me, are you a student?"

"Yes."

"If you're a student, and your father pays me to tutor you, then you've got to be objective. Understand? Be exposed to different points of view. You follow me?"

"Yes."

"That's why I was interested to hear your father say Judea had won. Because it really has, you know. Even more than he says."

"Really?"

"What do you think this war is all about?"

"I don't know."

"Did your father tell you that the war between Rome and Judea was really a war between the nobility and the masses?"

"No."

"Well, it was. And that has been Christianity's great victory. A victory against the spontaneity, the vigor, and the basic instincts of the ruling classes. You know what humility, poverty, penitence, and the life everlasting mean, don't you?"

"Yes. I guess so."

"And how many times have you heard that the last shall be first? Doesn't your father say that at least every other Sunday? And how about Jesus telling the people that it was easier for a camel to go through the eye of a needle than for a rich man to enter the kingdom of God? That's why I made that little swap with you. To give you some of the sword. So you won't be poor in spirit. Because that's what has happened, at the expense of everything in man that is virile and strong. So you see what I'm trying to do? Keep you from the clutches of the humble. What good is humility if it smothers the self? That's what is happening to you. Self-abnegation! If we need anything it's more selfishness! You were asking me why I haven't married. Now do you understand? How can I marry a man who has no manhood? Oh, there were a few men left. Before the Revolution. In Russia. But that's another story. That 1917 aberration of Christianity. You know what the Bolsheviks did? They killed the last vestiges of the ruling class. They obliterated whatever was left of intelligence. And in its place—you know what they have put in its place? Religion for the masses. Christianity and Communism. They're brothers, you know. And now we have the vulgar masses ruling the country. Just like in America."

Her lips have parted, revealing teeth in what is perhaps a smile but the movement is too rapid to be certain. Nevertheless, an emphasis remains in the high arch of the left eyebrow.

She has turned on the stool, facing him now, the brush poised in mid-air. The sun glints the surface of the small golden cross and sends tiny daggers of light into the eye. The cross is trembling with minute reflections, quivering on its fine gold chain looped around her neck, trembling its horizontal arms on the white skin above her cleavage where it is chained to the pale texture of her décolletage.

In the middle of the picture are the visible contours of Her heart laid bare pierced transversally from right to left with a sword no larger than the heart itself. The handle of the sword is in the upper right-hand corner while from the sharp tip, where it emerges from the heart in the lower left-hand corner, three drops of blood are dripping, suspended, timelessly, one after the other—one on the tip, two dropping, dripping on the floor of the locker room where they form round, shining, red circles, on the flagstones in the garden by the fish pond, where the crow's blood dripping off the tip of his beak has left circular stains of something or other which must be blood because the now dry droplets (if indeed they are droplets) are clearly visible on the light gray flagstones all the way to the end of the garden where the crow is buried—where it was shoveled under with one final squawk. . . . The three drops are suspended, timelessly, one after another from the tip of the sword where it has pierced the heart— the red heart laid bare in Her chest—the picture of Her heart laid bare on the wall above the blackboard.

Chalk marks are visible on a hastily erased surface. Particularly salient are the pressure points of periods where a strong hand (or arm) has punctuated the sentences of the last dictation—dictating the clauses slowly, emphatically—repeating each one twice and no more until the end of the passage, until it is time to gather the exercises in spelling, redistribute them among the students, correct them, and assign each a suitable grade.

"Bah! I used to be good at this but you know, something has happened. Tony must be right. Jerking off and sleeping with women weakens the mind. All that sperm you lose. Comes right from the brain. It's not so sharp any more. I used to be among the first five. Remember? Look at me this week. Eighteenth. It saps the mind, I'm telling you."

Roger draws a circular target on the center of the corrected dictation and aims at it with the tip of his pen. The pen handle quivers from the force of impact where the tip remains imbedded in the wood of the desk beneath the paper.

"Roger!" The voice of Brother Polycarp is loud and commanding. Roger gets up, goes to the teacher's desk, extends his arm, palm upward, and holds it there, unflinching, while the teacher's arm descends three times with the ruler and strikes three sharp raps on the open palm. Roger returns to his desk, sits down rubbing his hand, shoulders hunched over the desk.

"Doesn't it hurt?"

"I don't mind."

She is wearing a blue headdress—a pale blue covering that is as serene as the expression on Her face. It is the heart that is bleeding, and the red contours of its design, transfixed by the sword's sharpness, are flickering with a hot insistent flame.

"Cigarette?"

The flame from the lighter licks the tip, chars it black, she inhales twice, and the slender, oval, tobacco-filled piece of paper begins to burn with a glow which immediately transforms itself into curls of pale smoke.

"Don't tell me you and your friends haven't tried it, hiding in the cornfields?"

She puts the cigarette down in the ashtray and resumes brushing her hair. A filament of smoke rises rapidly, breaks, and then disperses in the air in floating nebulous directions. It is a medium-sized ashtray, baked with a white glaze, in the center of which, in black letters, in an easily legible script, is written "Honi soit qui mal y pense." A decorative band of blue forget-me-nots curls along the edges of the white glaze. The filament of smoke rises rapidly in a straight line before it breaks and disperses in the air. The boy picks up the lighter next to the ashtray. It is a flat pocket model with the initials N.B. inscribed on the silver. With his thumb he depresses the hinged lever which activates the flint. A spark ignites the wick and a small orange flame appears spontaneously in front of his eyes.

A man is holding the flame. One of three doctors is holding the candle under the palm of the girl's outstretched hand. The flame of the candle has been burning for almost a minute now under the palm of the girl's hand and she continues to hold her arm outstretched, unmindful, it seems, of the heat. There must be a burn. No, there is none. The doctors are examining her hand—the same hand—and there is no burn. They are shaking their heads, unbelieving. To their great consternation the flesh that remained in contact for so long with the flame of the candle has not been damaged. They are shaking their heads, clicking their tongues, and raising their eyebrows. Such an event, they are saying, violates all the laws of medicine, physiology, and chemistry. How can a young girl stand the pain? Yet there are no visible signs of pain, because if there were, she would be suffering from third-degree burns. "There is no natural phenomenon to explain this mystery." Brother Polycarp pauses momentarily, takes a deep breath, and resumes. "Only God's intervention could have prevented permanent damage to her hand. Bernadette really *did* see and talk to the Virgin Mary and the Grotto of Lourdes where the trance took place *is* sacred. The Virgin's appearance is indeed reserved for the very few—a handful of the privileged—those destined to become saints. Witness the many miracles that have taken place there since—the hundreds of crutches on the walls and in the recesses of the cave—all the people, men, women, and children, whose faith has restored them to health—cripples who have been able to walk again—blind men to see, deaf-mutes to hear and talk—an infinite number of ailments reduced and vanquished through faith and the divine intercession of the Virgin. . . ."

A procession bearing lighted candles is approaching the Grotto. Old men on crutches are hobbling along trying to keep up with the even rhythmic treading of feet but, unable to do so, they stumble and have to be picked up by stronger arms. A young girl with a brace on her leg is being wheeled to the mouth of the Grotto where a special Mass is being said. The opening of the cave is charred black from the smoke of giant candles and suspended from innumerable hooks are crutches, braces, walking sticks, and leather harnesses. The assembled people are crossing themselves, watching and listening to the priest in his golden robes raise the Host above his head, while others, on their knees, arms outstretched in the form of a cross, are moving their lips in unison with the words being said on the platform. The Mass is finished and the special moment has come, at last, for those whose faith is strong enough to cast aside the crutches of their sins and suffering and walk again in the way of the Lord. The young girl is being helped out of the wheel chair and an older woman is taking off the brace.

She is being led with faltering footsteps to the altar where she is receiving the priest's blessing. The crowd is crossing itself and the miracle is taking place: the girl is now walking unaided and the jubilant multitude cannot contain its joy. The girl is walking and the Virgin has again performed Her miracle. The people are saying, "Hail Mary, Mother of God . . ."

"Marc . . . Marc . . ." Roger is punching him in the ribs. Brother Polycarp's voice is saying, "Marc, you will write out the following sentence one hundred times: 'I will pay attention to the lesson.' "

I will pay attention to the lesson. I will pay attention to the lesson. . . . One hundred times, tediously written, laboriously copied, faithfully contrived to satisfy the exigency of the punishment.

"Dad. Have I ever been baptized?"

"No. Why?"

"No reason. Just curious. Will I ever be baptized?"

"The Protestant Church believes in making baptism a meaningful experience. That's why we wait until you get older. So you understand what it means. Maybe after the war we can take a trip to Jerusalem. Then if you want you can be baptized there. That would be a splendid and appropriate occasion. But there's certainly no urgency in the matter."

The small orange flame is burning on the tip of the lighter. Slowly the boy runs the index finger of his left hand through the center of the flame. It bends slightly, yielding to the passage of the finger, then straightens out again and rises vertically to a sharp point. The base of the flame bulges evenly and feeds the movement of the burning tip. The boy again runs his finger through the flame, more slowly this time, making an effort to control the reflex movement of his arm. But the pain jerks his hand back and he begins rubbing it with his thumb. The lighter itself is now too hot to hold and he puts it down on the dressing table by the ashtray. A long ash has accumulated on the smoking tip of the cigarette. The finger is hurting and there is a red spot just above and to the right of the fingerprint whorl.

"Stick it under the faucet."

The cold water reduces the pain but the river is now carrying him downstream. He is being carried downstream by the swollen, mud-colored, cresting river. His head emerges and submerges with the rough tossing of the waves and no one hears his cries. No, he is standing in the middle of the river. The water is flowing gently around his legs while the man dressed in camel skin pours water over his head. Water is dripping from his nose and lips—down his neck and chest—clear cleansing water—quietly purifying —gently washing away the hurt and the burn and the stains now dripping into the sink and flowing downstream forever.

The river loops around itself, flows through the countryside, under the bridge in the distance, and beyond the bridge it channels a gorge in the mountains. Beyond the mountains it is fed by innumerable tributaries, widens, and descends to the sea where, shorn, split, and parceled, it colors the blue shore for miles with its spreading yellow silt.

The cross is not exactly yellow. More of a beige, perhaps even ocher. But it looks darker because of the longitudinal grain in which the particles of dirt have accumulated.

"Imagine the task of pouring the ocean into a hole in the sand. Imagine the vastness, the depth, the magnitude of the ocean and then imagine the smallness—the insufficiency of a tiny hole into which, if it were possible, the ocean might be funneled." Brother Polycarp reaches into the folds of his robe, takes out a handkerchief, blows his nose, and puts the handkerchief back somewhere inside the recesses of the black robe. "That is the meaning of 'forever.' Of the eternity of the impossible, or of the possible."

A small boy is digging a hole in the sand, digging a round hole with a square tin shovel, digging as far down as his little arms will reach, bringing each shovelful of sand to the surface and carefully placing it in a pile by the hole. He runs to the sea and scoops his red pail full of water— carries the pail full of sea water back to the hole, and pours the water into the hole. The water is pouring in an even stream. The hole in the sand is almost full now and the boy is going back to refill the pail. A wave surges forward foaming around his ankles as he bends over scooping the sea into the pail. The water is clear and rippling with tiny granules of floating and swirling sand. He pours the sea into the hole and the liquid stream hisses, spurts, and foams. With time its shadow moves from left to right— moves imperceptibly with each trip to the sea—shifts its radius around the center of the hole—and becomes a solitary spoke revolving on the sand until the elongated line has formed an angle of 180°. The hole in the sand is not yet full. The sea is still rolling up the beach while the small boy, holding the tin shovel in his hand, and no doubt tired by now, is sitting on the sand facing the setting sun. He is crying, but the sound of his cry is not audible. Even the waves have crystallized and are suspended, motionless, like the seagull caught in flight.

Marc hands the picture back to his mother. She puts it into the album and turns the page. It is snowing outside and the mountains in the distance rise above the expanse of white fields. "That was a good summer. Remember? You almost learned how to swim." The log in the fireplace is spitting and hissing. "Your father thinks we might be able to get a cottage again this summer." She is handing him another picture. "I love the sea. That's you but even smaller. . . . No, you weren't always crying. But you were afraid of the water. It was the bathtub at first. Afraid of running down the drain I guess. Every time we pulled the plug . . . Oh hello, Nadja. Come in. Marc and I have been looking at some pictures. Beastly weather, isn't it? No, you're not disturbing us. Really. Have some tea. . . . Please . . . Cream or lemon? Marc, honey, run out in the kitchen and get me another lemon. I was telling Allan the other day how fortunate it was for Marc, and for us too, to have you move into the extra room. You have no idea what a load it is off our minds. Marc running across town . . . Thank you, honey. Those late trips back."

"You never know what dangers lurk on street corners after dark."

"Exactly. And I kept telling Allan it's not fair to have Marc walk all that distance alone in the cold."

"It was more fortunate for me too. Now I can help Marc more. Can't I, Marc?"

"Marc! Really now! I sometimes wonder where all your manners have gone."

"That's all right. He's making excellent progress. I had forgotten how much a young mind could learn."

"Oh, I think I hear Allan. Allan, darling, you're just in time for tea. And I was telling Nadja, or rather, reiterating what progress Marc is making."

"Hello, everybody. Nadja. Ruth is right, you know. Without your help Marc could not have gone back into his own grade. You have no idea what a help you've . . ."

"More than happy to oblige. Really. I love working with Marc."

"Yes. Marc is a good boy. He's been through a lot. But then that's probably not a bad thing. God willing, he'll make a better man for it. I sometimes think children should be protected from certain realities. But the war has made much of that impossible. Marc is a serious young man. Aren't you, Marc? . . . What are you reading, boy? . . . Sorry. Hold it up . . . A little farther. Light is bad. A little farther to the left. *The Pioneers*. How do you like it?"

"O.K. But not much happens. I wish all the description would end."

"Excellent study of early frontier life though. But I grant it's not *The Last of the Mohicans*."

"Is your room warm enough? The furnace has been acting up with this awful coal we get. Allan called the repair man. What did the repair man say, darling?"

"He'll be here tomorrow morning."

"This is a dreadful time for it not to function properly. I don't know what we'll do when this supply runs out. When there's no more."

"Don't be upset on my account. Please. I have a lovely hot water bottle. All my own. To keep me warm. Besides, you forget that my blood would keep a tiger warm even in Siberia."

"Ha, ha. I suppose you're right. I remember your father. Never wore a coat. Even on the coldest days. Not that Istanbul ever got that cold. But it does snow. And once a century even the Bosphorus freezes."

"You used to know Miss Bozshevska?"

"Sure, boy. Mr. Bozshevsky was one of the Russian refugees we helped when I was doing relief work in the twenties. A splendid man. Really a splendid man. And Nadja was just a little girl. And you weren't even born. A great chess player too, he was. Taught me a number of superb moves. Did he teach you too?"

"No. It's not my game. I was much more interested in my dolls. And my music, of course."

"Yes. I'd forgotten. You used to play beautifully. On that old piano we borrowed for your father from the Mission. Remember the way the porter carried it up the driveway all by himself? On his back. Bent over double. An incredible performance really."

"You could come down here and play, if you wanted to. Couldn't she, darling?"

"Why, yes. Of course."

"No. I'd be bothering you."

"No bother at all."

"You're too kind."

"Not at all. Marc won't play. And it's here. Please feel free to use it whenever you want to. As for me, I've got to go. Please excuse me, but I have to rework part of my sermon for Sunday. Will you all come to hear me?"

"Of course we will, Allan. What a thought! Don't we always!"

The album of pictures is lying open on the couch. The white border accentuates the identity of each snapshot. A very small child is sitting on the beach facing the sun. He is holding a tin shovel in one hand, a pail in the other, and he appears to be crying. But the cry is probably being muffled by the wind and the waves. Besides the boy is no longer crying. He is pouring sea water in a hole in the sand, and the sun, like the seagull, is racing from one horizon to the other.

"Those are good pictures, aren't they. Nothing like a camera to capture the present. Then you can show them to your grandchildren."

"I'll be off too. Thank you for the tea."

"Don't forget to let us know if you need anything. If your room gets too cold, I mean."

"Don't worry. I have my father's blood in me. Don't forget now, Marc. If you get cold I'll give you a transfusion."

Her laugh echoes in the hallway—her mocking, melodious laugh, that makes the blood rush to his ears.

The face in the mirror grimaces, showing teeth. The eyes squint, closed now, practically, into half-moons. The mouth is grinning, grimacing, no, the face is expressionless except for the redness spreading along the right cheek as far as the chin. A hand appears in the mirror and slaps the face. The cheek tightens and the hand slaps again and then again while the redness on the cheek spreads as far as the chin. A fist is hitting the chin: one, two, three times, and now the right side of the face is red. Fingers are touching, rubbing the cheek and then the fingers turn on the faucet, moisten the hands, soap them, wash and soap, rinse and soap and wash and rinse again. Cold water is splashing the cheeks, rinsing the mouth, spitting, rinsing, and swallowing. Then the hand turns the faucet off and wipes the face vigorously on the towel. An index finger turns the light off and in the dark there is the door, the desk, chair back, bed post, and the bed covers—the cool clean sheets of the bed free of the pungent fragrance of her body, free of arms and legs and the twisting circular motion of her hips—cool clean sheets and the stillness outside, transpierced by the distant shrill whistle of a train, followed by the rolling, rumbling, reverberating wheels that fill the night's silence. Silence that is a non-silence now rolling along the tracks and clicking over each and every railroad tie. It devours the distance between the telephone poles, appears and disappears through the cracks in the car. The moaning has subsided now and the crushed tormented bodies are resting in a kind of semi-sleep—a coagulated torpor tunneling the night—a disjointed convalescence until hunger fastens itself to the smell of excrement—the unyielding odor of excrement bonding the limbs and bodies into a fluid mass—writhing, flowing, coalescing the motion of entrails and the odor and metamorphosis of hatching flies.

Maggots explode—the sun and the blinding, burning, incandescent circle of fire flames ever closer, bursts the eardrums with hot trembling thighs, and the night, and the nightmare fused in the throat split the cry—in the stillness of the room—the wakefulness—the sheets—the tingling thighs and the eyes wide open now, staring at the invisible ceiling.

"We are Hitlerists and Roger is a Jew."

Tony is organizing the group to play a new game of tag.

"The Hitlerists are on the right side and it is our duty to chase Jews. Roger, you get a head start. I'll count to fifty. O.K.? . . . Go!"

Roger runs into the woods. . . . "forty-eight, forty-nine, fifty. Here we come!" Flames of yellow crocuses dot the fields and, although the grass is spongy from the late spring rains, running is easy and fast and satisfying. His knees and ankles are carrying him rapidly through the field of crocuses, to the edge of the woods, but instead of going in with the others, he skirts the trees to the right, and follows the slope, to the bottom of the hill. A narrow path at the end of the meadow leads to a gully of tangled vines where the hut is hidden.

"It's me. Marc. You O.K.?"

"Yeh. We can sit here for a while. Then I can run off again."

"This hut isn't bad."

His eyes are adjusting to the light inside where, on a wooden crate, Roger is smoking a cigarette.

"Where did you get the butts?"

"Snitched a pack from my old man. . . . Here . . ."

Marc takes one, Roger lights it for him, and then Marc sits down on the other crate. The boys smoke silently, not inhaling, sucking on the cigarettes, holding the smoke in their mouths, blowing it out through round protruding lips, watching the smoke drift upward through the cracks in the boards.

"How do you like being a Jew?"

"I don't mind. Somebody has to be one. What would Tony do if he didn't have someone to chase? Besides I'd rather be a Jew than him, any day."

The boys puff on their cigarettes.

"I got another letter from Mara. Want to read it?"

"Sure."

Marc takes the letter out of his hip pocket, unfolds it, and hands it to Roger. Roger reads the first page, turns it over, and reads the other side. He hands it back to Marc.

"Well, what do you think?"

"I guess she loves you all right. But I don't know about the rest."

"What do you mean?"

"You know what I mean! That bit about feeling closer to you inside the church."

"What's wrong with that?"

"Nothing's wrong with that. It's just that maybe I wouldn't go for it." Roger takes a puff on his cigarette, blows the smoke out with an audible rush of air, drops the butt on the ground, and steps on it with his shoe. "I guess it's about time for me to get going, or they'll be wondering where we are. Besides we don't want them to find our hideout." He stoops down, his body fills the narrow opening of the loosely jointed boards, and then there is only the light in the doorway and the sound of feet running along the muddy bank of the stream. Mara's handwriting fills the pale blue page with a neat, legible, slanting script.

Marc dear,

Your letter was wet from the rain by the time I finally retrieved it but I could still read it in spite of the blurred and running ink. Instead of putting it in the crack outside the garden wall I have a new idea. Suppose we use the twelfth pew on the far right aisle of church. It would be so easy to just reach under the cushion instead of feeling like a thief every time I walk around the corner looking to see if anyone is watching. Besides, I would feel so much closer to you inside.

But your letters scare me sometimes. I wonder if it's the you I know. That's why I'm afraid to let my parents see them. And I feel so wicked deceiving them. If it weren't that I love you so much I couldn't stand the duplicity. Really I couldn't. We're both so young to be writing love letters like this. I wonder if we ourselves know what we really want.

I have to be sure, really sure, and I could never give myself to anyone unless it was for good. Love is such a spiritual thing that I could never sully it. I even feel guilty kissing you sometimes. Not while I'm doing it, of course, but after, when I think of the wicked desires of our bodies. Oh, Marc, Marc, why is being in love so difficult? If I could only be strong and resolute like you. It would be so much easier. Help me to be firm. Please be my everlasting Rock!

Your loving Mara

Voices from the hilltop beyond the trees are calling "Roger" and "Marc"; voices that sound like those of Tony and the boys; voices which are mingling with unfamiliar ones farther away, beyond the river, no doubt, where the shepherds watch their flocks. A stone crashes through the branches of a tree and then another one whirrs through the air and plops into the stream. No doubt now. Another encounter with the shepherds. Marc folds the letter, sticks it in his hip pocket, and darts out of the cabin. He is running up the muddy bank and as he runs he pulls a slingshot from his pocket, untangles it, and loops one end over the first knuckle of the center finger of his right hand. His eyes are looking for a rounded stone of medium-sized proportions. The top of the hill is now visible less than thirty yards away where, in the clearing, the boys are twirling slingshots over their heads.

Marc joins the group. A stone is whirring through the air, whirring nearer with its invisible momentum, whirring until the thud and sudden impact of its flight have stopped. He picks it up, examines its contours, weighs it in his hand, and places it in his sling. He is whirling the sling over his head in slow even ellipses, deliberately breaking his wrist at the beginning of each revolution. He runs forward as the speed of the ellipses increases and moves his body into the throwing motion of the arm. The stone disappears with the familiar whirring sound. Marc waits, listening and scrutinizing the shapes of the enemy on the other side of the river. A series of invectives is followed by the thud of another stone, and then another, until the air is full of temporary pockets of noise. Then the two sides exchange insults involving mothers, sisters, and aunts. The smaller boys are gathering stones and piling them in little heaps.

The larger boys, after picking up several, and fingering their weight, select the right one. The stones are whirring sharply again, back and forth, scuffing the bark off trees, thudding the grass or crashing loudly through the leaves and branches of the trees.

"Up yours."

"Fuck your mother."

"Your sister too."

Neither side seems to know exactly who, how, or why these fights erupt except that, honor and virtue demanding vindication, the battle continues until one side, out of boredom, or fatigue, or because the sheep have wandered off, breaks contact and the groups disperse.

The bluish smoke is rising in a straight steady filament from the burning tip of the cigarette. It curls and then disperses in random floating wisps. She has turned on the stool, facing him now, the hairbrush poised in mid-air, while the sun glints the surface of the small golden cross. It pricks the eyes with tiny needles of light. The cross is trembling with minute reflections, quivering on its fine gold chain, trembling its horizontal arms on the white skin above her cleavage where it is chained to the pale texture of her décolletage.

"May I have it back now?"

"Please let me wear it a little longer."

The vertical segment is probably one foot long while the horizontal arms, slightly above center, are much shorter. It is more or less a standard wooden cross, with few specific distinguishing characteristics except that it has been hanging for many years now on the wall above the blackboard.

"Polycarp means many fish."

"Who told you that?"

"Haven't you heard of Saint Polycarp?"

The cork bobs again and the line tightens in his fingers. Marc begins reeling it in with both hands until the large, shining goldfish emerges from the flat surface of the pond —body and tail wriggling and twisting in the air—held wriggling several inches above the jetty while Roger removes the small sharp hook from the mouth, then drops it slithering into the pail of water. It swims around several times and then stops, gills opening and closing.

"How many goldfish do you think there are?"

"I don't know. Maybe a thousand. Maybe more."

Roger baits the hook with a half worm and from the torn section, through which the sharp, curved tip of the hook has passed, oozes a reddish brown mixture of earth and blood. He tosses the weighted end into the water and the two boys watch the ripple expand around the now motionless cork and disappear into a wide circumference. Marc lies down on his stomach on the wooden platform, puts both hands in the water, spreads his fingers, and cups his hands. He wiggles his fingers gently and soon white, red, and mottled goldfish rise to the surface and begin tickling his fingertips—gently nibbling on the end of each finger until with a sudden forward extension of the arms he grabs for the fish that has swum closest to the opening of the cupped hands. The fish scatter and Marc tries again, wriggling his fingers, waiting patiently for the nibbles, waiting for a fish to swim within the easiest position for an abrupt catch. The forearms extend again, the two hands are closing fast and there is a slippery firmness between the index and middle fingers. He is holding it tightly, tightly until he drops it with a faintly audible splash into the pail.

"Why do you want so many?"

"I'll put them in the bathtub with underwater archways."

"Yes. But why so many?"

"I don't know. So they won't get lonely."

"Fish don't get lonely."

The two boys are carrying the pail with short, running steps. The weight forces them to stop every hundred yards to rub the handle's red indentation on their fingers. The pussy willows are waving furry branches in the warm sunshine and somewhere, from the green foliage of a willow, echoes the sound of a cuckoo. Marc imitates the bird after it has stopped and, in the interval following his imitation, are heard five distinct cuckoos.

"Is it true that cuckoos lay their eggs in other bird's nests?"

"That's what Polycarp says."

"And that the foster mother feeds the baby cuckoo?"

"That's what he says."

The boys walk another hundred yards, then set the pail down, unevenly. One of the fish splashes over the side. Marc bends down, scoops it up from the dust in the road and drops it back into the pail. He rinses his hands in the water and wipes them on the side of his pants. A villager, perched on the rump of a donkey, stares at the two boys. The donkey's hooves raise muffled puffs of dust around its ankles. Farther down the road a throng of people is cheering and waving palm fronds and branches. No, there

is no throng, just the villagers on their way to market.
When Marc reaches home all the fish in the pail are still
alive.

"But, Mom, it isn't fair!"

"I just finished telling you. If Miss Bozshevska wasn't
living with us you could use the guest bathtub."

"But I want to keep the fish."

"If you can't be reasoned with, I suggest you go to your
room for a while. You can put them in our bathtub tonight. But tomorrow they go back."

She is in the dark hall, her form outlined in the light of
the open door.

"I don't mind fish in the bathtub."

"But it's such an imposition."

"Not at all."

She goes into the bathroom, puts the plug in the drain,
and turns on the cold water.

"Go get the fish, Marc, and let me see how many you
have."

She helps him put the fish into the tub but in doing so
they bump heads. She laughs, rubs the side of her temple
with the palm of her hand, and reaches for another fish.
There is the roundness of her breasts on either side of her
cleavage. The fish drops over the side of the tub with a neat
little splash. She bends over again to reveal her cleavage—
soft and pliant now under the pressure of his fingers—soft,
smooth, pliant, and yielding. She is whispering "Not here."
He puts the last fish into the tub where, with the others, it
swims around and around with fast flicks of tail and fins.
Some of the fish remain near the surface opening and clos-

ing their small round mouths, hardly moving at all, just opening and closing their mouths, reaching for the greater concentration of oxygen near the surface.

He takes the cigarette. The steady filament of blue smoke is pale and vacuous at first, and then dark black and billowing with the distant and delayed sound of explosions. The smoke rises high into the air where the upper wind currents are dispersing it in a southerly direction. The fires and the explosive redness on the horizon are not visible now, by daylight. There is only the redness of the Easter eggs hidden in the green grass and the eager running of bare legs. Then there is the challenge of egg tips to determine the day's strongest egg: orange eggs are cracking blue eggs and blue eggs are cracking yellow eggs and yellow eggs are cracking green eggs, well camouflaged in the grass. The muzzles of guns are also hidden in the bushes. The children are playing tag over the broken eggshells lying in white, purple, green, red, and blue fragments. Little mouths bite into the round shiny whiteness of an egg, chew the crumbs of yolk that adhere to the teeth and lips—teeth which are leaving a bitten half-egg outlined in white and yellow. There is an occasional red stain on the white egg protein where the Easter pigmentation has seeped in through a crack and colored the inside of the shell.

The boy reaches into the crow's nest, fingers the eggs, grasps three, and carefully retracts his arm from the thorny edges of the nest. He cups the eggs in the palm of his hand and examines the small black and white flecked oval shapes, more gray than white, in the total mottled effect, as they drop, one by one, from and in between the branches of the tree and break moistly on the ground in a wet yellow gelatinous splat. Roger and Marc congratulate themselves on the seventy-sixth crow thus annihilated that spring afternoon—seventy-six fewer black cawing pests to plague the countryside with their pestiferous habits and obnoxious presence. The pussy willows are waving furry buds in the warm afternoon air, and in the distance, the call of a cuckoo echoes five times from the green foliage of another season. Seventy-six fewer crows, though, to blacken the countryside with their cawing. Not only that, but twenty-four fewer magpies not to chatter like machine guns in the early morning.

Two airplanes are trailing the wail of their sirens across the sky. Their fendered landing gear and jointed wings give them the appearance of huge birds tearing off fragments of landscape. There is surely a black cross, outlined in white, on the body of each plane.

The bullet makes a hole in the center of each one. The holes widen to encompass the crosses. Twin trails of smoke are streaming from the tails of the planes. Tongues of fire spurt from the engines as the planes begin their plunge to the ground. Fire and smoke envelop them as they explode, hurtling fragments away from the black center. No, the crosses are intact and the only hole is in the triangle. The screaming of the sirens is receding, following the small flying dots of two imaginary lines. The clicking of the railroad cars is also receding, fusing the parallel and interminable lines of steel into the cry—the cry emanating from a point where the ties are no longer visible.

The two boys are walking on the rails. They balance

themselves on the narrow bands of steel, race along the shiny, endless, elongated tracks, and step occasionally on a wooden tie after losing their balance. They dart into the woods in pursuit of some noise, then return to the tracks and the game of running at top speed by only stepping on the ties, faster and faster, until Roger, stumbling, sprawls over the bed of sharp granite stones beneath the rails. There is a cut on his knee and the blood is running down his leg. He wraps a handkerchief over the hurt. Heavy railroad spikes are embedded in the ties. The square nailhead is holding his feet together and the blood is trickling from the hole. Lymph is now oozing from the wound on his flank, but the blood over his eyebrow has coagulated. There is an inverted crow's nest on his head. "Seventy-six crows and twenty-four magpies is a respectable average for one day. Wouldn't you say so?"

"Have another butt."

"Don't mind if I do."

The match flares brightly, the tip ignites, and the familiar odor of tobacco smoke curls in his nostrils, then wafts into nebulous bluish puffs. ". . . Why is being in love so difficult? If I could only be strong and resolute like you, it would be so much easier. Help me to be firm, be my rock, for together we must be faithful to the Commandments." Marc folds the letter and puts it back in his pocket.

"Well. What do you think?"

"I guess she loves you all right."

The two boys puff silently on their cigarettes. When they have finished they carefully step on the butts, put five grains of Sen-Sen in each of their mouths, rub their fingers with green grass, hide the pack of cigarettes in a tin box under some branches, and then stoop through the low door of their cabin.

Spring is in the air. The pussy willows are bursting into furry buds. The warm winds waft over the green wheat fields, while in the mountains the snows melt into trickles, run into rivulets, and cascade into waterfalls where the fish spawn in the pools. The late afternoon sun drops over the horizon, airplanes fall out of the sky, the crows descend into the trees, and the shadows stretch over the country-side. There is no magpie, now, lying under the pear tree and the insects are not buzzing over the pears. The branches are snowing white petals while in the willow the naked baby cuckoo is pushing little birds out of the nest.

There is the sound of snoring on the other side of the wall and she is asking him to get under the covers and not catch cold. He is lying next to her and she is fingering his sex. The head is opening and closing, flicking its tail, suck-ing in the air, scaling the radiance of hard sunshine, push-ing its way now into the hole, swimming around and around in ever widening circles from the center of the cork bobbing up and down, oozing now like a wet sponge, and falling, falling away, unable to maintain the hard brilli-ance of the first scales, falling out now, rolling over on his side with a tired: "I can't. Not tonight."

"Why not?"

"I don't know. I just don't feel like it."

"You're not angry with me?"

"I'm not angry with you."

"Why have you stayed away these last few months?"

"I don't know."

"But you're not angry with me now?"

"No. Not now."

"Are you sure?"

"I'd better be going."

"No. Please not yet."

"I'd better."

"Please wait a little bit."

The pillow is soft and on the other side of the wall there is the sound of hard, labored snoring. A dog barks somewhere in the distance and the bark is answered from some equally distant place. Her fingers are rubbing his cheek and lips, curling into his hair and around one ear. A cat begins to yowl outside under the window and her hand is now rubbing his chest. No, there are two cats lurking in the bushes hissing at each other and, as her fingers move up and down his body, the hardness returns. The meowing cats have run off into the woods and Marc is trying to go, but she has pushed the covers aside and has now enveloped his hardness with her lips and tongue. A star is shining distantly but very brightly, coming closer now, slowly, increasing its speed, magnifying its brilliance, as it descends from the night, focuses on him, concentrates its lactescence on the point of him which is hovering with exquisite pain, rushes in through the window and explodes into black fragments. The fragments are hurtling back into space. He is running now, stumbles down the stairway, goes out the kitchen door, out into the night air and moist cold grass, and spreads the sign of the cross under the Milky Way. One arm reaches toward the sky while the fingers of the other clutch the inaudible cry forming in his throat.

The grass is cold and wet with dew. The body is trembling and shivering—trembling under a sky that is alive with stars—the stars themselves trembling in the precarious distance—lights raining out of the blackness of space with a dimension that is suffocating the lungs, pulling at the roots of the eyes and roaring in the ears of time. Wet blades of grass under the fingers reach for the stars and the distance of the separation plucks at the root of rotating galaxies. The sky's semen fertilizes the axis of the Milky Way. Eyes, transfixed, are poised unblinking on the white shape of the moon that is rising over the trees, illuminating the garden shadows, irradiating the murmuring noises of the night, closing the harsh distance, trailing a white diaphanous gown with each approaching step, and the movement of outstretched arms. She envelopes his head with the whiteness of herself and the faint rustling of innumerable veils.

"Mara."

"Sh-sh-sh, my love."

"Mara."

"It is I, Nadja."

"Mara."

"Let me take you back. You'll catch your death of cold."

She lifts him, carries him over the trees, bears him aloft on the wings of innumerable birds, soars in the ether, higher and higher, toward the hunting grounds of the moon, nearer and nearer to its pale luminescence, all black now, lost, vanished, and dropping, falling, falling silently and interminably, forever, backward into the whole of the night, through the vastness of space, beyond the receding womb of light and stars, into the oozing miasmic continuity, more rarefied now, sharper in its outlines, less fluid and suddenly crystallized into the jagged summits of the Himalayas frozen and motionless in the blinding light of the sun.

He is naked in a landscape where even the wind has frozen into a tunic of epidermal pain as piercing as the sun's indifference. The world is static and time has been arrested. The only motion in space is registered as the contraction of skin over the bony protuberances of ribs. He is being allowed one lick of the tongue on the frozen granules of the summit. No forward motion possible now, only the body receding into a black vacuum, backward into the oozing, miasmic morass, feeding on a protoplasmic sea from whose depths emerges the torment of unimaginable nothingness, reversing time and, in so doing, eliminating hope, because the total reversibility of time in the vortex of a spinning helplessness is the black wing of doom screaming through the beaks of pterodactyls, tearing the body, clawing it to the winds, visibly dispersing the nerves and arteries as they disentangle and float apart, flowing and receding into the expanses of an endless and universal emptiness.

The waters of the protoplasmic sea are green and translucent, irradiated by the yellow bands of a sun hovering in primordial proximity; spindles, clearing toward the poles, split, multiply, and differentiate into a specialized organic continuity that swells the fibers of the species, follows the

convolutions of the matrix, feeds the blastospores of birth
and the infinite rivers of blood coursing the consciousness
or unconsciousness of breath and the wind animating the
deep foliage of summer, the persistent, elongated, high-
pitched, continuous grating sound that rasps in the stridence of its own making long after it has stopped and the
silence has folded inward on itself. In the aftermath of its
very absence it resumes a consciousness that comes to the
ear in a thin, slender, needled ribbon of sound.

The sun is hanging directly overhead and it is hot now
but in the night beyond the opening is the high-pitched rasp-
ing of the locust. The shadows on the wall are moving,
walking perhaps, whispering, hovering, sitting now, three
shadows, three heads looking, eyes looking . . .

"Are you all right?" Mouths open and close. "Marc, are
you all right?" Words . . . perplexed eyebrows, voices
ask, wonder, speak, demand, and coax. Hands tuck in the
sheets, rub the forehead, wipe the moisture, and turn off
the light. There is the sound of tiptoeing. It leaves an emptiness pockmarked by the mandibles of hornets, wasps, and
yellowjackets. Meat is hollowed, devoured, and consumed
in the semitransparent flights of sharp, nervous wings;
bodies tunnel under the skin, pour venom into cells that
swell to the bursting point, and then explode in a motion
so slow as to negate the evidence of the cataclysm.

"How are you, boy? That was quite a scare you gave us."

"O.K. I guess."

"Sure. You'll be all right. Never heard you say so much
at one time. Something about John the Baptist and a mountain. Who was in the desert, by the way. Not the mountain.
But you'll be up and around. A few more days."

He is wearing camel skins around his loins and he is standing on the summit. He is pouring water on the boy's head from an earthen jug but the water has frozen into an icicle. The ice is covering the boy's face which is still visible behind the transparent layer. The ice has immobilized his head as well as the arm of the man holding the jug. Neither person is moving. There is only the vast silence and the vertical bar of ice joining them together. A young girl carrying a lighted candle is floating up the side of the mountain, coming nearer now with her flame, standing in front of them, holding the flame to the ice, melting it into a trickle that is running off the tip of the boy's nose. The man's arm is pliable again and his lips are moving. The girl's face is raised toward the sky as she watches the descent of the bird.

The bird envelops the trio with its wings and carries them off to the rolling pastures. The hills are alive with a green luxuriance sprinkled here and there with crimson chrysanthemums and yellow-eyed forget-me-nots. The patterns form a harmony of color which echoes the plumage of the singing birds. The golden crests, crimson wings, and long tails of the pheasants blend with the lavenders and blues of the peacocks, while the birds of paradise, balancing themselves on the lower branches of the trees, are swaying in breezes of sunshine.

The insolent chatter of a magpie is breaking the dream apart, splitting the melody, tearing the colored rhythms into the black and white rattle of a machine gun. The magpie, balancing its tail in the wind, is perched on a branch in the pear tree. The bullet slides into place, the lock clicks, and the butt of the rifle nestles against the striped shoulder of the pajamas. The magpie is in the sights now, its black and white wings still visible in the white blossoms of the pear tree. There is a sharp report, the kick of the butt, and the bird which is falling from branch to branch in an uneven, inevitable descent.

The magpie is lying in a heap on the ground while the delicate white petals torn loose by its fall snow over the bird and illuminate the countryside.

It has been snowing all day—one of those winter storms during which the whitest flakes descend, multiply, and melt in your eyes as you try to catch one on your tongue. Millions of snowflakes are covering the countryside with white. The snow lies piled on the needles of fir trees, slopes the valleys, hides the contours of the hills, narrows the streams, and etches the tree trunks in black. The snow has covered animals, people, and houses from whose chimneys the blue smoke of wood fires curls upward into the rapidly freezing night air. The first stars are beginning to shine.

The men, idled by the storm and the indolence of a Sunday afternoon, leave the animals, leave their women to tend the fires, and go, as though propelled by some invisible force, to the tavern in which the fumes of red wine, spilled on the counter and on the mud-tracked floor, blend with the strong odors of wet sheepskin coats and fur liners. The men drink and exchange views in terse, laconic statements. During the week they talk to the animals or, with lifted faces, sift the information of the sky and the wind and the rain; they have strong callused hands which have felt the grain and the moisture of the earth and which know the seasons and the planting rhythms of growth. The snow has covered the fields and will now protect the winter crop from the cold and, God willing, it will be a good harvest in August.

But other men are also drinking. And the heady vapors of strong wine are mixing with the muddy tracks of fear and loneliness and suffering and hatred, mixing and brewing violence behind the red eyes of those whose vague faces are scrutinizing time and whose fingers are playing with the heavy glasses at the bar. The glasses turn and turn and turn, leaving multiple circles of red wine that overlap on the acid surface of the zinc. And the mud inside, and the wine, and the unarticulated thoughts argue themselves, midst the smell of steaming sheepskins, into loud angry voices, into raised arms and fists, and into the violence of a walking stick that descends, splintering, on a gray fur-lined cap. Nobody sees the sharp blade plunge through the sheepskin.

It is almost dusk now and the man is moaning that he is going to die. He repeats the words, saying that he is dying, stresses death's inevitability, insists that this is the end, and the stream of words with which he is covering his fear envelops the heady vapors and nods the heads of the men circled about him. The pool of blood on the floor, black now from the shadows, is creeping toward a table leg; the man's groaning is weaker and a doctor, since there is no doctor in the village, has been summoned, but the messenger is probably still on his way and besides, what speed can you make over snowbound roads on horseback; and somebody has thought of a hospital but the hospital is even farther than the doctor and besides, how do you stop the bleeding, and if he would only not moan about dying it would be better for everybody. But the unassuaged fear of the body repeats itself until all the sound has trickled onto the floor, around the table leg, and only the lips are murmuring a consciousness which is still in everyone's ears; but at last even the lips are still and the only sign of life is in the propped-up body and in the eyes, the bloodshot eyes, staring at the star that is visible through the open door.

It is one of those winter storms which occur slowly and silently. It accumulates deep layers of snow over animals, people, and houses and, when it is spent, the blue smoke of wood fires curls straight up into the rapidly freezing air.

The white petals, torn loose by the bird's fall, are no longer snowing from the tree. Nor have they covered the body of the magpie. The wind catches a long tail feather and lifts it in the air. The wind is also blowing the white petals, blowing the bees from the blossoms, blowing the pollinated stamens into tiny green granules of fruit, blowing the warm sunshine over hard pears and blowing summer juices that will soon bulge the sweet ripeness under the yellow skin. But now, it shakes the unpicked, fully matured, overripe pears to the ground where they lie rotting, half eaten by worms and insects. A soft pulp is draining into the ground with the raining autumn leaves, carpeting the lawn with yellow. The earthworms chew and digest the leafy smells and then excrete them vertically and horizontally before the birds catch their long, resistant, rubbery carcasses and slip them down their throats. The magpie drops into the freshly dug hole and, as the shovel pushes the earth over the feathers, the pressure of the metal edge pushes the wind out of the bird's lungs and it makes one final and, it seems, angry squawk.

The sling is whirling over his head in slow even ellipses. Each revolution and each deliberate break of the wrist is accelerating the momentum. He is running forward now, releasing the stone with a final flick of the hand and wrist. The stone takes flight and whirrs in the direction of the shepherd boys. Invective follows, then a stone whirrs back through the air, whirrs nearer and nearer until it hits the ground with a sudden and invisible thud. The stones are whirring sharply now, back and forth, falling sporadically and at random at varying distances, scuffing the bark off trees, thudding on the mud, and crashing loudly through the locust trees. Suddenly, the impact of a hard round whirr is visible, the head jerks back, but the impact is orange.

The scar on the side of the head has healed and the whirring blackness has gone but there is the raised portion of skin under the fingers where the hair is not growing on the slit of new tissue. The doctor is patting him on the back and telling him he is indeed a fortunate young man to have received only a glancing blow; yet the hour and time of day does not seem right. "The injury was epidural and we were able to drain the clot."

There is a dull pain on the side of the head covered by the feel of gauze bandages. "What time is it?" It is morning but it is raining and the curtains are pulled and it is hard to tell what time of day it actually is. A nurse shakes a thermometer, sticks it in his mouth, and holds his wrist with three fingers while looking at her watch. She writes on a chart, walks briskly in her starched white uniform, removes the thermometer, holds it up to the light, replaces it in the small narrow container of blue liquid, smiles efficiently, and then walks off on crepe-soled shoes that squish prophylactically on the shiny surface of the brown linoleum floor.

"The headaches are not so frequent now. Just on certain days. Then I have to lie down and take several aspirin until the dizzy feeling disappears."

The magpie is moving, elliptically, in rings round and round, higher and higher, yet forever backward, falling into the hole of night, falling into and beyond the chasm, receding into unconsciousness.

Black leathery bodies detach themselves from the domed ceiling, spread their wings, spray the cave animals with an acrid mist of ammonia that rains tiny droplets of rabies into the mouths and nostrils and sharp teeth of predators, contaminates the countryside with cries of mad death— squeaks the grimaces of their satanic faces, flaps the wings of doom, and darts evil eyes and sharp pointed ears into the crevices of night.

Yes, thousands of bats are now leaving the mouth of the cave, flying toward the big orange disk of the sun, whirring the air with their wings and bodies etched in black, a nervous metamorphosing cloud emanating, evolving, rising, billowing, falling, covering the sky with a webbed blackness, blotting out the sun, chewing it off the horizon, multiplying the night into millions of peeing bodies that are now exploding from the mouth of the cave.

The bats are flying in formation, flying together with the tips of their wings almost touching. Through the openings shine fragments of sky. But the wings are spreading night even as the siren's screaming sends jagged oblongs of pain diving out of above, dropping projectiles that whine long before their impact. And time, arrested, resumes finally again on accelerated heartbeats, but more slowly now, torn apart by a gaping hole. Slowly, fear and anticipation breathe more easily until the next screaming descent catches in the throat and immobilizes the swollen eyeballs that stare, listening to the earth's gravitational pull.

"There are two kinds of sin: mortal and venial."

The enemy arrives first by tank and on foot and then by truck, by car, and by motorcycle. Shoulders and helmets bristle with the even rows of rifles. In the back of armored vehicles, the muzzles of their guns etch themselves against the sky in diagonal black lines. The side-cars of motor-cycles bounce unevenly along the rough dirt roads. The splashing of mud has stained the black boots and the gray-green uniforms—the thousands of uniforms now setting up camp in neat wooden barracks with red geraniums flowering in wooden windowsill planters.

"Thou shalt not kill."

The soldiers have occupied all the hotels, have requisi-tioned private homes, cars, villas, buildings, fields, and bicycles. They have taken the land, the bread, the shoes, the coats, the gasoline, the airports, and the railroad sta-tions. They have appropriated everything movable and im-movable alike—shifting, transferring, transposing fruit, vegetables, animals, and people—all moving north— passing north through the railroad stations—cattle cars full of lowing cows and tightly packed bleating sheep.

The bells hanging around the sheep's necks are tinkling in the morning air as the flock moves over the contour of the pastureland. The lambs chosen for slaughter have red dye-marks on the white wool of their back and sides. They are nibbling the grass with a clever curling motion of their gray, almost black tongues, and a short jerky stroke of the head and neck. The shepherd is playing on his flute as he walks the flock while the goat, with his arched horns and black hair, leads the sheep through the stream. The dogs also wade through the water, lap it with long red tongues, lick their chops, and then clamber up the steep banks. The sheep are following the lead of the goat toward the green grass on the other side.

"Hurrah! . . . Hurrah! . . . Hurrah! . . ." The battle cry echoes and reverberates from every corner of the school yard. The students are shouting in unison following each sudden motion of the director's arm and fist, arm and fist moving upward above his head, arm and fist outlined, suspended independently at a right angle, gesticulating violently with each new hurrah, demanding that every lung swell into a full unanimous cry, molding the students into one emotional whole, forcing cohesion, violating their independence, eliminating doubt, assuring volition, constructing the emotional climate of order and subservience and adherence to order and authority.

Each hurrah conjures the image of soldiers stranded without ammunition on a mountain top—soldiers surrounded by an enemy inching forward from boulder to boulder—soldiers without ammunition desperately raising the bodies of the dead high above their heads to hurtle them at the enemy below. The enemy is thinking that the resurrection of the dead means the invulnerability of the enemy on top. The enemy below abandons its siege and flees crying in horror—unable to confront the attack of the dead—invoking Allah's assistance and fleeing from such miraculous power while the defenders, huddled and exhausted, collapse around the tattered remnants of the flag implanted on the summit. No, the soldiers stand triumphant and jubilant, thundering their victorious cry from mountain to mountain with every long rolling and resonant "Hurrah."

The angle of the director's forearm guarantees the victory and supremacy of the image—the picture that is in every history book, on the face of stamps, and which is a part of every grandmother's folklore: the image of victory concentrated in sound—the "Hurrah" capable of animating the vision, of solidifying resistance, of peopling the heart with pride and the indefatigable determination to resist and fight to the end in spite of hunger, sickness, weariness, and pain. No, victorious and full of glory in defending the fatherland. There can be no golden age without the zeal and support of the people. You are the people. *Hurrah!* We are the people and our hearts are like one, beating and pulsing the life force to the remotest corners of our nation. Sometimes even beyond. No, only to the borders; only as far as the people are one of us. . . . We do not attack. We defend. . . . We consolidate. . . . We are working for the good of the people. Hurrah! . . . Hurrah! . . . Hurrah!

One-two, one-two, one-two, hup-two-three-four—the one-two voice of the gym instructor blends with the sound of marching feet. The double row of students is marching around the football field, practicing, exercising, drilling obedience and control, refining its ability to turn, stop, start upon command, following the will of the man in charge, doing exactly what he wants because this is good exercise and discipline. Cannot lead unless you learn to follow. Obedience is a cardinal virtue. Honor your father and your mother. Respect your teachers. Your elders know best. Fear God. . . .

The parade is moving down Main Street while the sound of marching feet accentuates the blare of trumpets, the oompah of the bass horn, and the beat of the drums. The flags are waving in the breeze, the spectators lined along the streets are cheering the students, four abreast now rounding the corner, pivoting around the inside man, band playing full blast, the blue uniforms of the students moving briskly in a continuous symmetrical stream of heads, bodies, arms, and legs following the beat, stepping high now past the main platform on the square, faces turned sternly to the right, eyes on the main figure, shouting "Hurrah" three times at the given signal. Each rectangular and separate unit honors its school, cries out with the voice of one giant lung—multiplied—heads turning left now, facing the direction of the marching column, past the main square along the trolley tracks. The blue student uniforms blend with the shiny band instruments whose metallic luster fills the ears with the sound of honor and glory, quickens the heart of the crowd, draws a tear along the wrinkled cheek of an old woman, lifts a small child high on its father's shoulders, whirls the skirts of young girls, and puckers provocative whistles from the lips of the nonmarching boys.

But there is no tear now on the cheek of the old woman —the little girl is holding her father's hand—the heart of the crowd is not exhilarated—and the watching eyes are expressionless as tanks, chains, and wheels rumble through the main square, followed by the long muzzles of the artillery and the dark shapes of gunmetal, followed in turn by the armored cars and trucks and the tramping sound of boots scuffing the cobblestones in even, patterned, rectangular rows of black.

The soldiers are not marching now—they are standing around the railroad station—facing the crowd—rifles pointing at the crowd—keeping the crowd away—they will shoot, no doubt, if the crowd moves into the station from which the cries can be heard—from the boxcars stifling the cries. The guards will not allow the crowd near the side tracks where the voices of pain are tearing holes in the air. A guttural order is heard, then the clanking of couplings, and the hissing of steam. Wheels begin to move the train with a gathering momentum and the cries, blending with the clicking of the tracks and the creaking of the cars, vanish in the distance with the smoke.

Yellow stars are visible on men's lapels and on the gray of women's coats. Yellow stars identify the wearers as sons and daughters of David. And even as the chosen descendants are stopped in the street or lie in bed at night waiting, with their eyes open, another trainload is pulling out of the station—pulling out with the smelling viscous mass of flesh articulated with layers of bone. The sound of the wheels accelerates over the tracks, clicks the ties, reduces the distance between the telephone poles, and the up-down-up and abrupt renewal of the flowing motion of the wires, interrupted by the vertical presence of each pole flicking by in a continuous fluid intermingling, blending, and separating of wire strands.

The train tunneling through the night crushes the bodies, bonds the limbs together, coalesces the motion of entrails, and tenderizes every patch of skin. The bats are now flapping their wings, sharpening their black claws on the railroad ties, tearing the ties apart, scattering them to the winds, and carrying them off to build nests in which they pick decaying bits of flesh from their incisors with the sharpened tips of tibias.

The people lined along the streets are waving their flags and cheering the marching troops, four abreast, now rounding the corner, pivoting around the inside soldier—boots scuffing the cobblestones, stepping high past the main platform of the square—stern helmeted faces turned to the right, eyes focused on the leader, saluting the king bat who raises one wing in a sign of recognition and smiles through the interstices of pointed teeth.

The heat of the fire can be felt through the open door of the furnace. The flames are dancing over the coals, transformed now into a burning mass which is framed by the square edges of the door. It is a negative picture in which the white edge is dark while the figures, if there are any figures, are illuminated by the flames forever renewing themselves and feeding upon the supplies of combustible material being forced through the opening.

The body of a woman is entering the mouth of the furnace. She is lying nude on a metal grate and, as the door closes, the flames lick around her thighs and loins. The body of a boy is also being rammed, feet first, into the furnace. The stokers are shielding their faces from the heat blasting through the open doors. Smoke is now rising from the tall chimneys while, in the outlying fields, the crows are making small tracks on the newly fallen snow.

The flames are dancing over the yellow mass of coals. The figures, if indeed there are any, are illuminated by the flames renewing themselves and feeding upon the shovelfuls of coal being dumped through the opening. The edge of the shovel digs into the supply of briquettes, the handle swings around until the metal sides find the incline of the door, tips upward, and the coal slides through.

"But how do you know how much to put in?"

"Depends on the weather. It's fairly cold today so I put in three. Other days you'll need only two, or maybe one. Every few hours. Then set the heat at seventy-two. Stoke it, get rid of the ashes, and you're all set. Or, rather, do everything backward in that order. Be conservative with the coal though. When this is gone there is no more."

"Is this the kind of furnace they threw Shadrach, Meshach, and Abednego in?"

"Ha! I doubt it. But what made you think of that?"

"I don't know. I just wondered if God could save them from a furnace like this one."

"I don't think it is up to us to question God's omnipotence. Remember, boy, the Jews were the chosen people."

"But assuming we were the chosen people and someone threw us into a furnace, would God come to our rescue?"

"I suppose He would, son. I suppose He would. If your premises are right."

"But if He doesn't."

"Nonsense. God always does what is right."

"Is Hell as hot as the fire in there?"

"You certainly are full of strange questions today. Are you feeling all right?"

"There is a Hell, isn't there?"

"Yes. There must be a Hell. But as for the heat, I suppose the fire in the furnace is as good a comparison as any."

"But if Shadrach, Meshach, and Abednego didn't get burned up how do we know people in Hell suffer if they don't get burned up either?"

"There is a Hell, my son. Otherwise living has no meaning. A Heaven too. The just must be rewarded and the sinners will be punished. There is a Hell all right, but perhaps its dimensions do not always correspond to the sensations we are familiar with."

"Will I go to Heaven?"

"It wouldn't surprise me. Lead a virtuous life, believe in God, and even though you walk through the valley of the shadow of death, as the Psalm goes, the Lord will be thy keeper."

"Even if I'm not baptized?"

"Of course. What silly questions!"

"But . . ."

"Come on now. I've got to get going. It's half past already and you have your lesson to get to. We'll both be late. Let's get a move on."

The smoke rising from the chimney in a steady filament curls abruptly and redirects itself in random floating dispersions. The smoke is rising into the air in a steady, continuous swirl, pale and vacuous at first and then dark, black, and billowing. The crows take flight, flap their black wings, and propel their heavy bodies in a flat trajectory over the newly snow-covered field while the bluish smoke rises rapidly in a straight filament from the tip of the burning cigarette.

"You know, Roger, I had a funny dream."

"Funny ha, ha, or funny peculiar."

"Funny peculiar. I dreamt that Miss Bozshevska was being burned in a furnace. And then after they put her in, they pushed a boy in too. I couldn't see the boy's face. And then there were others, but I just saw the face of Miss Bozshevska."

"And then what."

"And then they closed the doors of the furnaces. And the furnaces were really hot because the men were sweating and they didn't have any shirts on."

The flame of the match licks the tip of the cigarette and the bluish smoke rises, curls abruptly, and spreads itself in a variety of floating dispersions. In the middle of the ashtray the inscription reads, "On y soit qui mal y pense." She has turned on the stool, facing him.

"Don't just hold the smoke in your mouth. Inhale. Otherwise you look like a girl. Here. Like this. Take a puff. . . . Now breathe in. . . . There . . . The first time is always the hardest. Your lungs have to get used to it. . . . My. You are coughing. . . . But you'll be all right. I certainly hate men who smoke like women. Dizzy? . . . Lie down for a moment. Might be a little hard at first. I was dizzy for days it seems when I first started. Even saw double at times. I'd look at one minaret and there would be two."

"Where was this?"

"In Istanbul. When I was a girl. One of my corrupt boyfriends taught me how to smoke. It was terrible in those days. For a girl to smoke, I mean. I'm sure my father would have paddled me. Though he was a pretty good father . . . One day we were both resting on the bed. This was earlier. In Moscow. Before we had to leave. I guess I must have been around eleven. He started fondling my breasts. Not that I had much . . . Not at that age. But they were beginning to bud. So he kept fondling my breasts. I just lay there. But then I got up and ran into the other room and told my mother. My father denied it all, of course. But I think my mother knew. . . . Besides . . . I don't know why I'm telling you all this. Are you feeling better? Still a little dizzy? Stay where you are. I remember about Moscow, though. It's funny what you'll remember. But I remember the mailboxes. They were yellow. Bright yellow. Like canaries. And the color sang out in the streets. And sometimes the sound would blend with the colors of the sky. At sunset. Beautiful skies they were. The sound of the sunset in the sky. But then it turned red. And now the sound is all the same and all the poetry is gone. And the song has faded into the drab mailboxes we have around here. That's why it doesn't upset me that Russia has been invaded. Because the people who run Russia now are nothing but criminals. Human residue which dared exterminate its intellectuals. And its ruling elite. So what do I care if Russians are being killed. It's the upper stratum that matters.

No. Russia will never be the same. My dear mother Russia where your eyes could turn blue just from looking at the sky. It's the blood that matters. And our blood is drying up in exile. Germany is Russia's only chance. A new ruling elite grafted onto the old stem. And if Germany loses the war then Rome and Greece will really be buried. And Judea will have triumphed again. Then won't the Jews and the Christians be happy. And as for men. I mean true men. They will disappear. A whole race. Castrated. Subservient to everything that would stifle energy, vigor, and everything superior . . . I'm sorry. I get carried away sometimes. . . . Particularly when I talk about my childhood. Do I sound bitter? I suppose I do. But it all fits into the pattern. Because without perspective you get drowned. You know what I mean? I always rant like this, don't I? You must get tired of listening to me. No? . . . Anyway. Sometimes I feel I do enough talking for both of us. Ikhnaton. Was it Ikhnaton? Never mind. He certainly would not have had to cut your tongue out to be one of his burial priests."

The sun, which is glinting the surface of the small golden cross, hurts the eyes with tiny piercing needles of light. The cross is trembling with reflections that quiver on the fine gold chain looped around her neck. It trembles its arms on the white skin above her cleavage where it is chained to the pale texture of her décolletage.

The wheat is swaying, bending, rolling, and unfurling like a sea of gold. The waves of summer are undulating its surface. She is lying on the bed now while the elongated, high-pitched, continuous, rubbing sound of the locust casts its stridence over the unfolding creases of her chemise. The black hairs of the triangle are now exposed to the insistent rasp of the locust. Flames lick the turbulent mass of hair while the hole opens to receive the shaft of sunlight that is reaching into the folds.

The flames are rippling now, forking and multiplying. The tongues, locked in the coals, are forking the design while the vigorously flowing tide crests on the elongated, high-pitched, continuous grating rasp of the locust.

He is lying with the fragrance of her hair in his nostrils, conscious that the circular motion of her pelvis has stopped. The sea of wheat is still now, while the cross, no doubt, is lost somewhere under the pillow. Only the fine interlocking segments of the chain are visible on a spot of her neck that is still pulsing hard. She kisses him on the ear, rolls him over, and reaches for a pack of cigarettes lying on the table. She puts one cigarette between her lips, picks up the lighter and gives it to him. He depresses the thumb-catch and a small yellow flame appears at the tip of the wick. The flame chars the end of the cigarette, she puffs on it twice, inhales deeply, and blows the smoke out with an audible rush of wind. He replaces the lighter on the small table by the head of the bed by the cigarettes. A camel is on the face of the pack, his two front legs slightly spread, one in front of the other. He is standing on the hot Egyptian sand on which in blue capitals is written TURKISH AND DOMESTIC BLEND. The yellow desert and the line of its horizon occupy the lower third of the picture. In the left background are three yellow palm trees on whose right is a pyramid, much smaller and, presumably, much farther away. The brown camel is situated exactly in the center and occupies approximately two-thirds of the landscape. Its one hump, arched neck, and head are clearly outlined against the sky which is rendered in white. The large silver letters of the word CAMEL are printed across the upper third of the pack. A second pyramid is on the right, perhaps equidistant from the camel and the trees. It appears to be much larger than the first but is, nevertheless, smaller than the animal whose tail crosses one of the pyramidal ridges near the summit.

"What kind of cigarettes are these?"

"American."

"Really? Where did you get them?"

"A friend of mine gave them to me."

"But how can anyone get American cigarettes?"

"Booty, my friend. Booty."

"I don't get it."

"It's like this. When an enemy is defeated and flees he sometimes leaves things behind. I got these from a German officer. Understand?"

The camel is standing in the middle of the desert and is much larger than either the pyramids or the palm trees.

The boy leans over on one elbow, takes the cigarette from her fingers, and bends over the triangular mass of hairs. He holds the cigarette between three fingers and singes one of the hairs. There is a slight sputter and the tip of the hair disappears leaving it noticeably shorter.

"Marc. You're tickling me!"

He singes several more hairs and there is now the distinct odor of their burning. She continues to protest but does nothing to interfere with his determination to singe the pattern of a small square within the larger outline of the triangle. She lights another cigarette and smokes it while he continues to singe each separate hair. The filaments curl and disappear within the burning tip. The burned square is almost finished now and she is asking him if he is going to sign his masterpiece.

But he is pressing the cigarette into the hairs—pressing down hard with his fingers—holding the butt in place with the palm of his hand—pressing down firmly over the mount of hairs. There is a burning sensation at the base of his palm but he is pressing the cigarette down hard into the hairs of the black triangle—pressing the burning end down into the skin beneath—holding the cigarette down with the palm of his hand—fighting her attempt to push him off, burning the triangle with his hand and the pain which is shooting up into his arm.

"Marc! Are you crazy?" She pushes him away violently. There is now an acrid smell in the air.

The Roman emperor is shouting that the Christians did it even as the flames etch orange shadows against the night and the people are jumping into the Tiber to avoid the heat and the crumbling walls. In the arena hungry lions advance toward the men and the women kneeling on the ground. But where is Brother Polycarp? The people are moving their lips and their eyes are fastened on the sky. . . . The wild beasts are tearing them to pieces and the crowds are roaring for blood. No . . . The airplanes are roaring in the sky because all the lions are now tame and they walk docilely beside the people whom they might otherwise be eating. The only roar left now is in the airplanes and the tall booming guns. It is the martyrs who are sitting in judgment and God is separating the sheep from the goats.

The orange flame on the altar is burning and flickering in the bluish haze of dusk. The music begins and the two female dancers step quickly and gracefully to the center of the open-air temple. Their bodies sway to the exotic music and their arm and finger movements blend with the rhythm of the stringed and percussion instruments. Both dancers are dressed in identical ritual costumes of gold, silver, and crimson cloth while one long white plume is attached to and waves high above their heads. The two plumes are swaying against the blue sky of dusk. On the horizon, across a verdant plain, rises the dark purple outline of a mountain. The bare feet of the women are following the regular intricate step of the dance. Their legs, their lithe bodies, and their arms are perfectly synchronized with the tempo of the music. They wed movement and sound so perfectly that the resonant noises of hollow drums and wood blocks seem to come from inside their hollow bones.

Each movement traces a line in space and each gesture of the hand completes the figure of an unknown hermetic formula. Their feet kick aside the robes, dissolve thought and sensation and prune, fix, separate, and subdivide the feelings of the mind. The folds of their costumes encircle the abstract rotations and the strange crisscrossing of feet, curve above their buttocks, hold them as if suspended in air, and prolong each leap into a flight.

The women's stratified, lunar eyes, like dreams, carry the spectators to the forest in a rush of animal and mineral meteors. Their bodies stiffen as though besieged by the frenetic dance of rigidities and angles, as if waves of matter were tumbling over each other, dashing their crests into the deep, and flying from all sides of the horizon to be enclosed in one minute tremorous portion of trance. The hands, like insects in the green air of evening, communicate the obsession, the inexhaustible ratiocination of a mind taking its bearings in a maze of unconsciousness. Their eyes roll and their limbs tremble. The music sways behind them and sustains the space into which their gestures fall so accurately. Their hands, wrists, and elbows seize the rhythm of the drums, accent it, and mold it into such precise lines that the alphabet splits stones and reveals the mutinous noises of the earth. At first the dance accentuates their separate movements, but gradually the bodies of the dancers merge, and the superimposed plumes alternate, back and forth, in opposite directions, then fuse into one continuous rhythm.

The Prince claps his hands three times, the dancers stop, and four black snake charmers with boas twined around their arms and necks appear and walk to each of the four corners of the stone platform on which the plumed dancers are now standing. A high priest, dressed in white and carrying a spiral of gold in one hand and a star of silver in the other, is coming down the steps of the pyramid. He advances across the flagstones that separate the pyramid from the square platform, ascends the steps, walks to the center of the platform, and raises the spiral and the star, holding them outstretched so that his body and arms now form the shape of a cross. The beat of the percussion instruments increases as the young girls resume their danc-ing, moving counterclockwise around the high priest.

The black-haired dancer takes the star and the blond one takes the spiral and together they begin the ritual marriage of the cosmic elements. The priest in his white robes retreats to the back of the platform and folds his arms on his chest. The bodies of the dancers blend again and the plumes wave in unison, as the four arms intertwine in a fluid, rhythmic, and graceful exchange of day and night. Then the two brides descend the steps of the platform, move swiftly to where the Island Prince is sitting, and offer him the symbols of their allegiance. He is now holding the spiral and the star, one in each hand, clasped arm over arm to his breast, while he pronounces the words of welcome, bless-ing, and acceptance. The dancing brides then sit down on the purple cushions by their master, the blond one on the right and the black-haired one on the left, and the feast begins.

The lions are gnawing the flesh of their victims even as the crowd continues to roar its approval. The eagles are now roaring like lions, spitting fire, and flying across the continent. The movement of the sun has indeed been accel-erated.

He draws one vertical line and intersects it in the middle with a horizontal one. Then he draws a shorter line at right angles on each of the four tips. The design wants to revolve to the right so he draws another one in order to compare the two. But the effect is the same. The sign wants to move. He then draws a star next to the swastika, but this design is not interesting so he takes a clean sheet of white paper and draws a circle in the center. In the center of the circle he draws the star and at nine, six, three, and twelve o'clock he draws a swastika. A star surrounded by four swastikas. The design is pleasing enough. He then draws a straight line that radiates outward from the circumference opposite each swastika. In between each of these four lines he draws four more, making a total of eight lines radiating symmetrically from the edge of the circle. The circle now looks like a small sun with imaginary sunbeams. In between each sunbeam, and at a moderate distance, he draws a star—eight stars in all. But the effect is static. In order to set the design in motion again he draws a short line at right angles to each sunbeam. Then he crumples the paper and throws it into the wastepaper basket. He takes a clean sheet.

Dearest Mara,

I called and called last night but you didn't come. Why not? Were you sick or something? I waited in the garden for almost an hour hoping you would come. I was at the usual place so you couldn't have missed me. Is everything all right? As I say, I called and called and then it started to rain. So I went home. But I am writing to find out if you are O.K.

I love you,
Marc

He is taking a clean sheet of paper on which he is again drawing the circle, the star, the four swastikas, the eight sunbeams, and the eight additional outlying stars. He could add an infinite number of stars and swastikas. Instead, he is coloring the stars with a yellow crayon. Nine stars in all: eight outside and one in the center. The thin lines of the swastikas now seem pale in comparison to the yellow stars. So he is giving each swastika an indelible blackness with repeated strokes of the pencil. Four swastikas in all—five if you count the circle with the sunbeams. He adds a short perpendicular line to each sunbeam and again sets the sun in motion.

Hornets are crawling over the pears—darting nervously over the fruit, nibbling the skin with their mandibles, and eating holes in the flesh. The boy is stamping on the hole, jumping up and down on the opening from which the hornets are emerging. He is running across the pasture now but the stings on his neck and ears are like hot stabs of sunlight. The insects are burning holes in his ears, burning his head into a black oval hollow cranium visible from the inside.

The black-haired bride and the yellow-haired bride are sitting down next to their Prince waiting for the feast to begin. But on the horizon, across the plain, the purple mountains are erupting. They color the sky with bursts of flame. The Prince, his brides, and the guests remain sitting as though transfixed.

"How about a game of chess, boy?"

"Sure."

"Which hand do you want—left or right?"

"Right."

"Black. You lose. I get the white."

The sound of her laugh echoes in the hallway and he can feel the blood rushing to his ears. But the pawns and the queens and the bishops and the kings are at last all in place and he is concentrating on the first move of her wrist

which is combing the shiny filaments of black hair—setting
up the sequence of moves that will capture the rooks and
the knights and the midnight blackness of her or is it their
embrace . . .

"What happened to your hand?"

"I burned it on the furnace."

"Let me take a look at it!"

"Really, Dad, it's nothing. Just a little burn from the
grate handle. You know. As I was emptying the ashes."

"What's wrong?"

"Nothing much. Marc has burned his hand on the furnace."

"Honestly now, Allan. I told you Marc wasn't ready to
stoke a furnace!"

"But, my dear. He is not a child any more. It's time he
learned some responsibility."

"Yes but not if he has to burn his hand doing it."

"Sometimes that is the only way."

"Oh, Allan. Can't you see he is still a child."

"Come here, boy. Let me take a look at that hand."

"Really, Dad. It's nothing. Just a little burn."

"Come here and let me see it! Your mother seems to
think it's important. Here. Take that bandage off!"

"Do I have to?"

"It does look like a pretty bad burn. How did you get it
anyway?"

"As I said. From the grate handle. Emptying the ashes."

"Looks as though you picked up a live coal."

"There now, Allan. What did I tell you!"

"Oh, Ruth! It's not as serious as all that."

"It really doesn't hurt at all."

"I think he's going to live. Aren't you, boy."

"I still think he has no business stoking the furnace."

"You don't want him to get soft lounging around the house all day. Like Nadja."

"What does Nadja have to do with it?"

"The burn doesn't hurt at all. Really it doesn't."

"I just think she could be helping you more than she does."

"But she is always helping Marc with his lessons."

"Yes. I suppose she is. Maybe that's what I'm objecting to."

"But it was your idea. Didn't you ask her to tutor him when school closed?"

"Yes. But I'm wondering if he doesn't rely too much on her now. That's why I thought . . . maybe . . . with the furnace . . . you know . . . some responsibility . . . your move, isn't it, boy?"

The black pawn in front of the king advances over one black and one white square. A white knight jumps out and stops in front of the row of white pawns. The black queen scuttles diagonally away from the king. Other pawns move, rooks advance, bishops plot strategy for the unoccupied black and white squares in the middle of the board, where the knights are jousting, until one of the kings falls, doomed by the intricate forces working toward his destruction.

"Too bad, son. That was a good fight. Better luck next time. It takes experience to become a good player."

"You're right about that."

"Like that question you asked me the other day."

"Sure. I remember."

"It takes time to get the right words. I tried to condense an awful lot of history for you. Sometimes I think it's not always meaningful. The first time, I mean. Anyway . . . What I was trying to say, badly perhaps, was that Christianity's counteroffensive to Greece's and Rome's militarism was a spiritual one. And the key word was love. Christ's teaching that we love our neighbors as ourselves was designed to lend the same kind of dignity to others as people already gave themselves. A famous philosopher once said that man unto man is a wolf. That was true once but, fortunately, it is no longer so. Or, perhaps, less so. For Christianity's impact has literally transformed the Western world. The whole idea of suffering as a redemptive force has given the world a new power with which to transform itself. And man's mark of dignity, which was once measured by his cruelty and strength at arms, is now measured by his humanity and tolerance of others. Am I making myself any clearer?"

"Yes. I think so."

"Anyway. We have a long way to go yet. And the final battle has yet to be fought. Figuratively speaking, of course."

"Miss Bozshevska says that's what this war is about."

"Well. Maybe. Though it's too early to tell. Her hypothesis is a good one though."

The crow lets out one squawk and falls to the ground where it lies in a crumpled heap. The hunter raises the gun to his shoulder and shoots the rabbit where it is now lying with its belly exposed. The impact of the blast has scattered a few wisps of fur. The snow is also covered with red stains of blood. The muzzle of the gun is still pointing at the insistent shadows between her thighs.

Dear Mara,
Why won't you answer my letter? Are you mad at me or something? Tell me what's wrong!

Marc

The end of the burning cigarette is singeing the triangular surface of her sex. It is singeing the hairs, burning a square within the larger outline of the triangle. The filaments of black hair curl and disappear within the burning tip. He is pressing the cigarette down hard with his fingers, holding the fire in place with the palm of his hand, pressing down firmly over the smoking mount. The palm of his hand is hurting now, burning, and he is fighting her attempt to push him off.

"Are you crazy?"

He is lying on the bed rubbing the palm of his hand, listening to the water in the shower. The eye must angle itself sharply up or down in order to see more through the narrow aperture of the keyhole.

"Mom, where's the soap?"

"Right where you left it the last time you washed your hands."

"But that's all gone."

"Don't tell me you've used it up already. Where has it all gone?"

"It gets the coal dust off my hands."

:: 141

"There's more in the kitchen. Under the sink. How's your hand?"

"O.K."

The hard granules of soap are biting into the dirt, foaming under the water, sliding the palms and fingers of one hand over the back of the other, rubbing, rinsing, resoaping, scrubbing with the brush, foaming the dirty lather, rinsing again, shaking the droplets off, wiping the clean hands on the towel and replacing the towel on the rack.

"Did you find it?"

"Yes, I found it."

"Hurry up, we'll be late for church."

The wind is chasing the March rain clouds, blowing gray wisps of material over the chimneys while the rain itself is sewing the sky to the roof tops, blending heaven and earth in a cold bone-chilling drizzle. The fine needlepoint of the rain is audible on the umbrella in a continuous, steady downpouring of droplets that occasionally drop a larger one whenever it detaches itself from an eave or a gutter and falls on the stretched impermeable cloth with a loud round plop.

Marc and his mother cross the street, go up the steps of the church, and pass through the heavy oak doors. His mother is now nodding to acquaintances even as she is folding the umbrella. The church attendant takes it and puts it on the rack where a long row of wet black shapes is already streaming puddles on the floor. The pool of blood is creeping toward the table leg and the moaning has subsided. . . .

"Let's sit over here." One, two, three, . . . ten, eleven,

twelve. "Here." Marc feels the edges of the folded letter in his coat pocket, takes it out and, as he sits down, slips it under the faded green cushion. His hand remains under the cushion and, as his mother turns her head, he retrieves another piece of folded paper. The church is filling rapidly and the latest arrivals, who have bowed their heads in silent meditation, are now opening their eyes and beginning to look around. The congregation is Protestant and there are no booths in which to confess sins and receive absolution. Some are listening to the organ music, others are nodding how-do-you-do from pews across the aisle, while still others are already putting an index finger in the hymnal, waiting for the service to begin. The organist has pulled out the stops now because the pipes are booming, moving the congregation to its feet, summarizing the familiar melody, announcing the end and then again the beginning as the words and the music swell from the pews, blend the voices of the men and the women, the boys and the girls, the old and the young, into a chorus of militant tramping feet, ". . . marching as to war," spreading the gospel of the Saviour, anointing the unfaithful. Mara's letter is now carefully spread out on the pages of the hymnal.

Dear Marc,

I am sorry I didn't answer you sooner. But I could not. Really! I could not! I got a letter from that awful woman who lives in your house. I can't tell you what she said because I can't believe that it is true. But I do know that she is evil and that if you have anything to do with her she will poison you just as she has poisoned me. Please tell me it is not true.

Your loving Mara

The high priest with his arms folded on his chest is watching the two dancers sway back and forth on the raised square platform. But on the horizon, across the verdant plain, the cone of the volcano is spurting fire and smoke. He is pressing down hard with the palm of his hand, pushing as hard as he can on the smoking mount. The camel in the foreground is standing on the yellow desert sand. His size accentuates the smallness of the two pyramids and the three palm trees near the imaginary line of the horizon. His head is under the C, his hump is under the M, and his tail is under the L. The letters from tail to head spell LEMAC. Separately and from left to right the syllables read CA, ME, and EL. There are five letters, not eight, and the pack of cigarettes is almost a perfect square. The letters ME are the same as those on the bathroom key. But the key easily fits into the lock, while the camel . . .

On the back of the pack the walls, domes, and minarets are the same color as the sand. The camel probably could not walk or fit through any of the doors or windows. The openings are colored deep blue, almost black, and the air inside is no doubt a cool refuge from the hot blazing of the sun. The camel would have to stay outside in the heat or perhaps he could stand under the shade of the palm trees. In any case, the doors of the houses would be much too small for him to enter.

His father is praying now, invoking forgiveness and assistance, in the name of the Lord, reading from the Bible . . . speaking directly to God without the aid of intermediaries, a spokesman for man's personalized contact with the Deity. He is reading the story of David and Goliath and how "David put his hand in his bag, and took thence a stone, and slang *it,* and smote the Philistine in his forehead, that the stone sunk into his forehead; and he fell upon his face to the earth. . . . Therefore David ran, and stood upon the Philistine, and took his sword, and drew it out of the sheath thereof, and slew him, and cut off his head therewith. And when the Philistines saw their champion was dead, they fled." . . . And because the Israelites, whom Moses led out of Egypt, were the chosen people of the Lord they prevailed over the Philistines. . . .

The marching feet are keeping time to the rhythm of the band; the red, white, and black banners are waving in the wind and the people, lined along the streets and standing on the sidewalks, are cheering the troops, four abreast now, as their boots pivot around the inside soldier, scuff the pavement, and step high past the platform of the square. Stern helmeted faces are turned to the right, eyes focused on the huge man brandishing the sharp reflections of the sun on the blade of a sword.

The giant is wearing a helmet of brass upon his head, and he is armed with a coat of mail, and he has greaves of brass upon his legs, and a target of brass between his shoulders. He is brandishing a sword which no ordinary mortal could lift and with it he is chopping off the heads of the Israelites. "They set fire to the Reichstag!" The heads are rolling down the incline of the cobblestones, rolling like dozens of bowling balls, and the people at the bottom of the street are running away, but many of them stumble and fall and are knocked over by the rolling heads.

Flames are leaping from the windows, are lighting the night sky, are illuminating the faces of the people. They are casting shadows on the walls of the buildings. A huge man wearing a coat of mail and a helmet of brass with a sharp, four-sided spear tip rising vertically in the air from the crown of metal, dominates the crowd. The lions are roaring again.

His father's voice is loud and clear. It fills the church, reaches the ears of the people, tells them to resist the oppressor, draws the parallel of David and Goliath, speaks in the name of the Lord against the godless heathen, and praises the partisans and the underground of all nations. He has never seen his father gesticulate so, his face become so red, nor his voice so loud. The congregation is still. Marc's mother is biting her lower lip. His father is speaking of a nation's inhumanity, of the violation of God's word and man's. He is referring to the trainloads of children nailed in the box cars. He is alluding to the fear of mind and body and to the stifling of justice and love and to the disappearance of those who dare speak against the beast, against the tyrannical monster, against Goliath. He is saying that men of faith must not be afraid to speak against evil, to resist evil, because God will protect the virtuous. "For I say unto you, the ungodly shall perish and those who seek to save their own lives shall lose them, but those who die in the name of the Lord shall live for ever."

At the back of the church there is a noise, the sound of voices, and the scuffing of boots. All eyes turn to stare at four soldiers stepping down the aisle, walking rapidly toward the pulpit where the minister is still speaking against the violation of human rights, and against the suppression of love. One man climbs the pulpit, grabs the preacher, and drags him down even as somebody in the front row tries to interfere. But the butt of a rifle sends him crashing to the floor. The men are now dragging his father up the center aisle. His shoes are trailing on the rug. He is trying to stand and walk but he is being forced down by the soldiers holding his arms. He is trying to say something but several fists are punching him in the face. His mother is stifling a scream with a clenched hand poised in front of her mouth. Invisible arms pull the oak doors wide open and the four green uniforms and the one black robe pass through. There is the sound of a slamming door, the grating of a gear, and the acceleration of an engine, followed by the interminable honking of the car. The aisle of the church is empty.

"Any word about your father?"

"No."

"I'm sure they'll let him go."

"You don't have to make me feel better. I know how it is."

"He was a very brave man."

"I guess he just couldn't stand it any more."

"Somebody had to speak out."

"But it was awful. The way they kept hitting him in the face. And the way they dragged him. I hope they didn't beat him."

"I love you, Marc."

"I know, Mara. It's no use. You don't have to make me

feel better. Professor Lubovny never came back. And you know what happened to your uncle."

"But we can pray for them."

"It must be hard on you having to wear this star all the time."

"It's better to wear it than not. If Uncle Aram had only worn his he might still be alive."

"But you don't know he's dead."

"No news they say is good news."

"I love you too, Mara."

"Now who's trying to make whom feel better."

"I wish there were some way of finding out! Why can't we find out?!"

"Sh-sh. Not so loud."

"I don't care who hears us. No. I'm sorry. Really I am! About the star too. They really fixed you, didn't they. The easier to spit on you. Nice little twist. Isn't it? . . . Well . . . Isn't it? . . . Why doesn't the giant fall?!! My father was speaking for you! But where's the stone? What happened to David's stone? They take my father and there is no stone. And it's all your fault."

"You really loved your father."

"He was my father."

"He was a brave man."

"What good is bravery."

"You don't mean that, Marc."

"Sure I mean that. What good is bravery?"

"I'm sorry, Marc. I'm sorry and I love you."

"But they've got my father. And you have no stone."

"We'll get a stone. But it takes time."

"Bastards. They're all bastards."

"Love is stronger than hate."

"No it isn't."

"You hate and then something inside you slowly dies."

"What do you know about it?"

"I know that Uncle Aram might not be alive. But I can't hate them for it. They don't know what they're doing. They're sick. And when somebody's sick you have to take care of him."

"They're mad! That's what they are."

"But somebody has to take care of them. Don't you see? That will be our stone!"

"Well, good luck. But don't die waiting for it to happen! . . ."

"Please, Marc. Let's change the subject. Here, read this."

"It's not true. Whatever she says."

"It's from Miss Bozshevska."

"The woman's insane."

"I know. But read it anyway."

My dear Mara,

You will no doubt wonder why I should be writing to you but since I am "au courant" of your correspondence with Marc and since I am very fond of him and therefore, by implication, of you too, I thought that information of benefit to you would, in a way, also be of service to him.

These are extremely difficult times as you are only too well aware. I am thinking of Marc's father and your uncle Aram and, it occurred to me, that since Marc does love you, if anything happened to you, now that his father is gone, the shock

*might be too much for him. Not that it will be any easier on
you since there is a certain inevitability hanging over your
head and not over his. But you are wearing the star and I
did want to tell you and your family to avoid being seen in
public, to scrupulously observe the curfew hours, and to do
nothing which might otherwise incur your enemy's wrath. For
all I know you might already be doing these things. If so, so
much the better. I merely wanted to caution you for your sake
as well as for Marc's.*

*I am no mind reader, of course. Nor am I an historian in
the scholarly sense. But I am something of an amateur
philosopher and I know the feelings of a class of people sometimes called the nobility, since I myself am one in exile. And if
it were not for our historical indifference to almost everything
that the Western world now considers important this war
might not have been necessary. But as I read the signs, a new
race of men is sweeping down from the north who consider
you (not you personally but the Jews) responsible for the
majority of man's afflictions. This, no doubt, has already
occurred to you too, since your father can no longer work
and his business and bank accounts are being liquidated. But
I wonder if all of you are aware of how serious the threat is.
Nor do I want to alarm you unnecessarily, but merely to urge
you to take the necessary precautions.*

*All I wanted to say was that the intelligence behind the
occupying forces may not rest until the operation to remove
Europe's cancer has been performed. What is taking place
now is a reversal of values and with it, perhaps, the reversal of
two thousand years of history. Do you follow me? Perhaps
not. Let me be more specific. The present Judeo-Christian
tradition insists, does it not, that those who suffer are good:
the poor, the impotent, the small fry. The sick, the needy,*

the pious have God's grace, do they not? On the other hand, the masters, the nobles, the strong, the cruel, the tyrannical, and the rich are, are they not, pretty much damned not to go to heaven—generally speaking of course. So maybe this war is, somehow, the payoff for old accounts—for the belittling of man's noble instincts, for the insidious way in which Israel has been taking its revenge on mankind ever since the first century. But the superior race has, it seems, at last taken stock that it has been corrupted from beneath, unknowingly. That they have, so to speak, bitten the hook of Israel's vengeance and been taken. Because that's what the crucifixion of Christ means, you know. That's what it was. A subterfuge, so the world would lower its guard. Can you imagine anything more subtle than a people which pretends to negate its own spiritual saviour by putting him on a cross? God crucified! Or the unimaginable folly of God crucifying himself in order to save humanity?

Because the symbol of the cross is all-pervasive. Is it not? It is everywhere. Not only in the churches. You see it in museums, in books, in cemeteries, on the remotest mountain passes, even around people's necks. Though why anyone would want a cross around his neck is beyond me. But fundamentally that's where it is. Whether modern man wears one or not. Anyway, the cross has triumphed and the masses have won. The flock is everywhere and everybody is trying to be a lamb. Humanity has been led by the nose for two thousand years by very clever goats who now seem to be becoming scapegoats. So you see you are part of the race of goats which has been leading the sheep and, in the meantime, profiting behind their backs. Rich men cannot enter heaven, you say. But your rich merchants have been the most successful who ever walked the earth. Well, the bells are tolling for the sheep now and it seems to me as though the blond warriors who have been suffering too long from the insidious poison of the Jews have a plan to right the balance.

Please do not misunderstand me. The last thing I would want is for any injury to come to you, though my sympathies inevitably are with the reversal of values now long overdue. Moreover, I am too fond of Marc, and the people he loves and likes, to wish you, personally, any harm. And if I seem to have digressed terribly, which I am afraid I have, it is perhaps my rambly self (ask Marc—he will confirm that side of me) which cannot dominate all the irrelevancies that frequently come to mind. But, remember, I have yours and Marc's interest at heart and the last thing I would want is anything to happen to either of you. Please accept this letter, therefore, in the spirit in which it was intended and may God protect you.

Yours sincerely,
Nadja Bozshevska

"I see what you mean."

"She is mad, isn't she."

"But she wouldn't hurt you. Not the way the Germans would."

The fish are swimming in the pond. The goldfish are swimming in and around the reeds and the towers and archways of the underwater castles. The shiny scales of the fish glint an occasional ray of sunshine which has (who knows how) penetrated to the greenish depths. The goldfish are swimming nearer the surface now and, as they angle their bodies toward the sun, the light catches and is reflected more frequently on the scales. Dozens of golden daggers are now piercing the eyes, pricking the retinas with pinpoints of light. The sun is whirling out of the sky, whirling dozens of nebulae into elliptical circles. Myriads of blinding crosses with broken arms are whirling out of the sky, whirling the scales of the fish, coalescing, fusing, expanding the flickering light runes, the arms themselves revolving into the giant orifice of a carp which is opening and closing, opening and closing, opening, swallowing, devouring, consuming, falling, slithering, sliding backward, down, forever, into the black, oozing, miasmic continuity of a protoplasmic sea—a sea whose green translucent waters are irradiated by yellow bands, spindles, cleaving toward the poles, splitting, multiplying, swelling into the fibers of the matrix, feeding the infinite rivers of unconsciousness, whirling cuneiform bird tracks into patterns of white, black, and red.

The flag is waving in the wind. The wind is flapping it swiftly, snapping the seams briskly back and forth in the strong current of air that has spread the cloth against the sky. The red cloth with the white circle in the middle, in the center of which is flapping the swastika. The black cross with the broken arms is snapping briskly back and forth—snapping, flapping, rippling, and crackling like fire.

There are clouds of orange smoke. The flames are illuminating the sky, licking the black with tongues of fire while the people are running, shouting, waving, and gesticulating. The reflected shadows of their arms and heads are like giants on the walls of the buildings opposite the conflagration.

The flames are dancing over the coals, transformed now into a white-hot burning mass framed by the square edges of the furnace door. The edges of the shovel dig into the dwindling supply of coal. The handle swings around, moves toward the hot open door and, as the shovel tips upward, the black briquettes slide into the burning orifice. The orifice is now spewing into the air. Clouds are rising high above the plain and raining ashes over the countryside. The eruptions follow in quick succession, rumbling the earth, as a side of the mountain splits and pours out a river of lava. No. The flames have transformed the burning mass into pale yellow vibrations framed by the square edges of the open door. The flames are renewing themselves and feeding on the bodies strapped to the frames of the metal grates. The grate is moving back and forth with a loud clanging noise of iron and the ashes are sifting into the ashpan. The round knob of the grate's movable wedge is bright and shiny in contrast to the sooty outlines of the furnace.

"Dad. Do I have to empty the ashes?"

"Good for you, boy. Teach you responsibility."

"But do I have to do the furnace. I mean. Can't I do something else?"

"Sure. When it gets warm you can weed the garden. And then you can help me build that retaining wall."

The wind is flapping the flag, flapping it swiftly, snapping the seams briskly back and forth in the violent current of air that has spread the swastika against the sky. The black cross with the broken arms is snapping back and forth—snapping, burning, rippling, and crackling—turning, burning, revolving, whirling faster and faster.

The goldfish are swimming around the reeds, the towers, and the archways of the underwater castles. Their shiny scales glint an occasional ray of sunshine that has penetrated to the greenish depths. The carp are swimming nearer the surface and, as they angle their bodies, the sun catches and is reflected more frequently on the scales. Dozens of daggers are now piercing the eye, alternately stabbing the retinas with pinpoints of light. The sun is whirling out of the sky, whirling dozens of black nebulae into round white circles. Thousands of black crosses with broken arms are reaching from the sky, coalescing, fusing, expanding the black runes of marching boots. No. Swelling the black robes of Brother Polycarp into the giant orifice of a fish. No. Into the black runes of revolving legs. Yes. Billowing Brother Polycarp's black robes into the huge mouth of a fish that is opening and closing.

Cattle cars are moving north. They are disappearing in the distance where the rails converge into the wail of the train's passing. Night fills the gaps between the ties. The grate, on which the boy is lying, slithers silently through the fish's mouth and falls into the hole of the dream, through space, beyond the receding womb of light into an oozing, miasmic continuity—colder now—more rarefied—sharper in its outlines—less fluid—and then crystallized into the summits of the Himalayas, frozen and motionless in the sun's brilliance. The boy is naked on the landscape and even the wind has frozen into a clinging tunic of epidermal pain as piercing as the sun's indifference.

"But you know, Marc. The thing I don't understand. Why they put children in the box car. If your father hadn't told me I wouldn't believe it. I mean that day in the station. When the trains were going through. Coming from the south?"

"That's what they said."

"Who."

"Those who heard them."

"Did your father hear them?"

"No. But people told him."

"But it's not human."

"What do you think they did? I mean the children."

"Remember that island in *Pinocchio* where the bad children turned into donkeys?"

"Yes."

"You don't think it's something like that."

"No."

"But what's the point?"

"Maybe there is no point, Roger."

"But there's got to be a point."

"Why?"

"You believe in Heaven and Hell don't you?"

"Yes."

"Well, I don't."

"So."

"So there's gotta be a point."

"I don't follow you."

"I just don't believe all that crap Brother Polycarp dishes out in class."

"What do you mean?"

"You know. About suffering for the redemption of mankind. Because I bet that train ride was no picnic. And if those children shrieked all night then either they did something wrong or there's no point."

"But what's Heaven and Hell got to do with it?"

"Now look here, Marc. If you believe in Heaven and Hell you can say, 'I don't understand it. But there's a point. Those who suffer will go to Heaven and those who make them suffer will go to Hell.' Right? At least that's what Brother Polycarp says."

"Yeah . . ."

"But if you don't believe in Heaven and Hell then you gotta find another explanation. And I never heard of children being nailed in a box car and shipped north. So either it isn't true, or else, there's something very strange going on which nobody knows about. And I just can't take all that nonsense Brother Polycarp dishes out."

"Why not."

"It just doesn't make sense."

"It makes sense to me."

"Yeah. I know. I've seen you cross yourself."

"I don't cross myself."

"Come on now, Marc. I've seen you cross yourself. When you thought no one was looking."

"That's not true."

"Come on now, Marc. I'm your friend. Remember me?

I'm Roger. You don't have to lie to me. Besides. I don't
care whether you cross yourself or not."

"O.K. Maybe you did see me. But not very often."

"You can cross yourself as many times as you want to.
I was just wondering why you would. Since you're a Protestant."

"I don't know. I just feel like crossing myself sometimes."

"Forget it. It's just that I don't understand how they can
do it. Because I keep thinking that maybe we'll be next.
Not you. But you know. Me and Mara and the others. It's
all like a bad dream. And I keep hoping we'll wake up.
It would be awful not to be able to wake up. Like your
dream of the bats."

"I know."

"To be stuck with the real thing. And not be able to get
out."

"I also dreamt I was swallowed by a fish."

"But not to be able to get out."

"How did you know I couldn't get out?"

Outside, the flag is waving in the wind but inside, a man
dressed in black robes is lying on a cot. His eyes are closed
and he is not breathing. Outside, a crow is fluttering
through the branches, limb over limb, down from the
leaves, falling to the ground where it lies crumpled in a
mass of black feathers. One feather is floating obliquely
and at wavering angles, to and fro, in its interminable
descent to the ground. There is a round hole where the
bullet has passed neatly through the crow's head. A bullet
hole that is a huge, monstrous, empty eye staring back

through the penetrable void. The feet are black and shiny and as smooth as fish scales to the touch. Not a heavy bird, but heavy enough so that the wings hang limply from the body. The body is swaying back and forth with every step. A trickle of blood is visible on the beak. There are three drops of blood on the flagstones by the fish pond.

The edge of the shovel is digging into the moist, puce earth. Digging. The hole is large enough now and the carcass of the crow (or is it a magpie) fits snugly into the ground. The air in the crow's lungs makes one final (almost human) squawk as the tip of the shovel pushes it down into the hole. Happily, the feathers are disappearing under the fresh mound of dirt. The sun has emerged from behind the storm clouds and is shining on the flag.

"Marc. Don't use up all the soap."

"But, Mom. How am I going to get all this dirt off my hands?"

"It's just that there's no more soap after this is gone."

"Remember that retaining wall Dad wanted me to build? Down by the pond?"

"I just don't know what we're going to do. The sugar is all gone. And there's no more butter. And the little bread we get is so wet and spongy it is only fit for pigs. I just don't know what we're going to do!"

"Roger said they were making soap out of old grease, ashes, and lye. Maybe we can try it."

"But must you use all we have now?"

"But they're dirty, Mom."

"Must you wash them so often?"

The cake of soap is biting into the dirt, foaming under

the water, and sliding the palms and the fingers of one
hand over the back of the other. Marc rubs, rinses, resoaps,
scrubs with the brush, foams the dirty lather, rinses carefully under the strong jet of cold water, shakes the droplets
off with quick flicks of the wrists, and then dries his hands.

It is a strange hand with its elongated worms—bait for
all kinds of goldfish, carp, and suckers. Strange fat worms
like the larvae of June bugs whose rows of concentric rings
band the body as far as the eyes and the mandibles. The
mandibles are opening and closing now, showing the hairs
around the mouth—opening and closing mandibular
hairy teeth—teeth exuding a brown stain—staining the
hand—spreading over it—covering the hand with a
brown, opaque, impervious excrescence. The hand is now
hard. Harder than the bar of soap which can be nicked
with a fingernail. A glove is going over the hand.

"But it's not cold, Marc."

"Sure it's cold." The glove is a light pigskin tan with
symmetrical dark pores stretched tight over the hand, over
the strange brown thing covered with the opaque impervious excrescence.

"Aren't you hot with gloves on?"

"No. I thought I'd go work some more on the retaining
wall."

"Why use your good gloves for that?"

"I just wanted to use the shovel."

"Wouldn't the garden gloves do just as well?"

The face in the mirror grimaces and shows teeth, the
eyes squint and close practically into half-moons; the

mouth grins yet the face is expressionless except for the redness spreading along the right cheek as far as the chin. A hand in the mirror slaps the face. The cheek tightens and the hand slaps a second and third time while the redness on the cheek spreads and covers the left side of the face. Fingers rub the cheek and then hands turn on the cold water. The water is pouring over the hands and fingers. The water is pouring over five wriggly worms and the worms are now reaching for the soap, crawling over the soap. The worms are now foaming at the mouth, foaming and slithering and washing down the drain, going down the round black hole in the middle of the sink, the white sink with the dark hole in the center, and at last the worms are going down. Close the drain now so they can't come back up and at last the hands are pure under the water foaming the soap, sliding the palms and fingers over each other, rubbing, rinsing, resoaping, scrubbing with the brush, foaming the white lather, rinsing again, shaking the droplets off, wiping the wet hands vigorously on the towel, and replacing the towel on the rack. But no, the worms will no longer wash off and the hand is one solid brown excrescence.

The slope along the north edge of the garden where the spring rains have washed away part of the lupine bed is steep, but the new retaining wall is beginning to take shape. The pile of rocks is now half depleted and, from the end of the garden, looking over the lawn past the pear tree to the house, the base of the rock wall is emerging above the level of the ground. The wall is at an eighty-degree angle, leaning ever so slightly in the direction of the house.

The boy is filling the space between the wall and the garden with the washed-out dirt, packing it even with the level of the stones, stamping on it with his shoes, jumping up and down and getting his shoes muddy. He then carries the stones, one by one, and places them on top of each other along the bank. The wall will be approximately fifteen feet long and two feet high, thicker at the base than at the top. The length of it has now been laid and the left side, as you look at the house, is already beginning to rise.

The garden gloves are covered with grass stains. The white strands of cloth are gray and dirty now, smeared with brown earth. What was once a white glove now has brown and green stains on it. The white, which is no longer white, is rather an insistent gray, even black in places from work that has been done in the garden where the dirt is much darker than at the edge of the lupine bed.

The boy is digging under the pear tree, removing the grass sod in neat six-inch squares and piling the squares along the edge of the hole. The rows resemble a retaining wall of earth and grass. On the other side of the excavation the pile of dirt is getting larger and more pyramidal as the hole gets deeper and longer. He is now inside, tossing each shovelful of earth out over his right shoulder, squaring off the edges, shearing the sides vertically, measuring the depth which is not six feet yet, but satisfied with the corners which form a right angle.

The excavation is finally deep enough and long enough. At the bottom there is a man with his eyes closed, his arms folded on his chest. The man is dressed in the black robes of a preacher and he is wearing the inverted white collar of his creed. The boy is now rapidly shoveling the earth over the corpse, covering the black robes and the white collar with chunks of dirt, filling the hole, pressing down on the diaphragm with the edge of the shovel. The pressure is forcing the air out of the lungs with one final loud squawk. The boy is jumping up and down, stamping his feet, getting his shoes muddy, and trampling the moist earth under each indentation of his heels. He carries a large stone from the pile and places it on the wall on top of the others. The length of the wall is now complete and, as you look at it, over the lupine bed (where lupine might have grown), the left side is slightly higher than the right. The white of the garden gloves is no longer white; it is an insistent gray, even black in places from work that has been done in earth in other areas of the garden—earth which has left visible stains on the minute stitching of the crisscrossing threads.

The needle is moving through the weave, etching its design on the white background of the cloth. Her wrist and fingers manipulate the in-and-out movements of the needle, and tighten the thread as her hand goes up and away from the delicate pattern outlined on her lap.

"Are you going to do all four tips?"

"No. Just this one. Do you like it?"

"Uhm . . ."

"I see. Never mind. But you could at least admire it. . . . Too late now though . . . Have you finished the poem?"

"Do I have to?"

"All you have to do is to pay taxes and die. . . . And obey your parents. . . . Isn't that why I'm here?"

"But I don't feel like it."

"Don't tell me you prefer your 'Dear Brother' teachers to me! Maybe I should wear a long black robe with the split white collar in front and heavy black wool stockings. Though I don't imagine the stockings matter much since you can't see them. It would be a lovely bit of subterfuge to wear sheer silk under the robe. And flat black shoes. And when I go out walking I could wear one of their bowler hats with the wide, flat brim. Would you like me that way? And we would of course begin and end each lesson with a prayer. Be very devout and all that . . . Did you say all your prayers last night? . . . I see. . . . Cat's got your tongue. . . . Of course we wouldn't make love. All very proper, proper. And then maybe you'll end up in a monastery after all. How would you like to be a monk?"

The needle is moving through the weave of the handkerchief, stitching the design on the white background of the cloth. The thread is being needled into the delicate pattern each time the length of shiny steel passes through the weave. The needle is now on the underside and it is not visible. The cross-stitching of the yellow pattern is almost finished. The needle reappears, then the eye, and the two strands of yellow thread. The eye is so small, however, that the thread barely passes through the opening. Yet it is of the thinnest imaginable and probably expensive.

The pack of cigarettes is lying on the table next to the bed. The camel looks well fed and muscular and he does not seem to be living off the fat of his hump. If he were scrawny and emaciated he might be able to fit into tight places but this camel is obviously a large one who would even have trouble standing under the shade of the three palm trees in the distance.

She needs a new thread. Soon she will be holding the needle up to the window. She is holding the needle in her left hand while, with the right one, she tries to pass the thread through the small hole. She is moistening the thread in her mouth and trying, once again, to insert the tip. Surely some light is still passing through the eye.

Dear Marc,

I had to write to you because I couldn't let you think I had anything to do with Mara's going. Particularly after the letter I wrote her. If I tell you that the letter was really intended for you, and not her, would you believe me? Perhaps not. Or it may be too late. And I admit I was angry with you for what happened. And part of the letter was in spite. That I admit too. But since talking between us was no longer possible and since I was afraid you might tear up any letter I might write you, I used Mara as an intermediary in order to get my last thoughts to you. I had to do that for your sake and mine, even at the risk of having my intentions misinterpreted.

And now that I am actually living with a German officer (the same one by the way who gave me the pack of American cigarettes), I'm sure you must think me doubly suspect. But that I can't help. I have at last found a man who is not only real but a kindred soul. You may laugh at this since I laughed at your relationship with Mara. But he really is an eagle. Serene, calm, aloof, and majestic when at rest, but when in bed he devours me with an absolute beating of wings and claws. And I am completely his, even when he is tyrannical. But his is an objective cruelty. It is a cruelty which is not afraid. Not a mask for other things. He is a god simply because it pleases him to act. He and I, together, shall produce beautiful children.

You too could be one of us if you would only let yourself

be. But you must forget me. *You must also forget Mara. I still have your little cross by the way and shall keep it as a souvenir. And in return you may have the sword. Use it to cut the bonds around you. Destroy whatever will not let you be yourself. I have at last found a man who is not afraid and he has given me insuperable joy.*

My deepest sympathy for Mara.

> *Your affectionate*
> *Nadja*

The ray of sunshine is now illuminating the room. Tiny particles of dust are crossing and recrossing the barrier of light (which is no barrier since it stops nothing, but merely suggests the outline of the visible), dancing back and forth, following the slight shifts in the room's air currents. A sudden turbulence swirls the dust particles and brings new ones to replace those which have disappeared beyond the barrier of the upper diagonal. The lower diagonal is absolutely parallel to the one above and it is only within this narrow band of light, no wider perhaps than six inches, that the disturbance is visible. It is impossible to blow the dust particles out of the light beam and, in spite of the effort, new grains appear, swirl, disappear, and evolve within the now decreasing violence of the movement.

The blizzard has been raging for two days. The snow has been swirling over the treetops, the branches, the bushes, the paths, and the roads, covering the hills and the black earth of the farmers' fields. All the fields are now white and the arable land, with its pattern of one field next to the other, is like a vast white checkerboard. The only suggestion of black is the presence of a flock of crows.

A fly has landed on the folds of the handkerchief, but the movement of her hand and fingers scares it off into the diagonal of light. The insect flies toward the window where it is now buzzing loudly against the lower right-hand corner of the glass. The light of the sky is outlining the center piece of the window which, in turn, is holding the four panes. The vertical and horizontal pieces of wood which intersect in the center of the window are visible only as dark segments of wood. The window is now alternately flashing four panes of light against the black outline of a cross. The cross is suspended in the middle of the sky. It is holding panes through which the sky is accumulating wind-heaved, billowing clouds that cramp the sun and push its light out of the heavens. Out of the tangled mass and the visible upheaval of the sky's original brilliance the blizzard bursts forth with a renewed and determined vehemence. The wind drives cold sleet into the eyes, needles them with pain, makes them water, forces the pedestrians to walk with their heads lowered and their backs hunched, forces them to bear the burden of the sky's anger, forces them to slip and fall and, always with bowed heads, to struggle back to their feet and onward, hunched, under the beating storm.

The snow drifts through the air, drifts the fields which are now white, covers the checkered fields now being outlined by the clever movements of her fingers and the sharp tip of the needle that is sewing the square outlines of a white weave on the larger square of the handkerchief. The trees along the farmers' fields lend a checkered effect to the snow-covered flatness of the region, interrupted, here and there, by the diagonal crossing of a road or the apparently aimless meandering of a river which loops around itself before it disappears under a bridge. The thimble is pushing the needle. Nimble fingers retrieve it, insert the tip and, with an apparently endless continuity, repeat the necessary and sometimes tiring motions for the elaboration of the final pattern.

It is one of those winter storms which occur slowly and silently over a period of days, accumulating many feet of snow, paralyzing all movement, spreading itself in deep layers over animals as well as people.

The man is moaning that he is going to die. The unassuaged fear of the body flows with the words, flows with the sound that has trickled onto the flour, that has inched up to and around the table leg. But the lips are quiet now and the only sign of life is in the eyes, the open eyes, staring at the star that is shining in the night on the other side of the door.

The father is not groaning any more. He is lying in the earth under the pear tree and the shovelfuls of dirt are covering his black robe. The boy jumps up and down, stamps his feet, tramples the moist earth with his shoes, and presses the loose stones down into the ground with the heels of his sandals.

No. He is not pressing them down. He is coming down the mountain path and stumbling on the stones. The sandals are made of leather straps and thongs which twine around his bare feet and toes. He stumbles and almost falls on one of the loose stones but with great strength retains his balance and continues down the mountain.

"All you have to do is pay taxes, die, and obey your parents."

The white teeth of the comb are still locked in the black waves. She has turned, facing him now, and the sun glints tiny daggers from the surface of the cross. The cross is hurting his eyes where it is chained to the pale texture of her décolletage.

"To die in a state of mortal sin!"

The flaps of Brother Polycarp's collar are flat and squared at the edges. The two white flaps accent his black robe.

The heat of the fire is coming through the open door of the furnace. Flames are dancing over the coals. The flames are rippling the surface of their duration, forking, multiplying, evolving, undulating their metamorphosis, consuming themselves in an endless succession of locked tongues.

"Dad, have I been baptized?"

A boy wrapped in a tunic of epidermal pain is licking the summit of Mount Everest.

"I'm Roger. Your friend. Remember? Besides, you don't believe all that nonsense Brother Polycarp dishes out in class!"

The arms of the cross are spread on her back now, under the fragrance of her hair. The skin of her neck, where the sun has been shining on it, is warm and soft.

The camel is walking through the arch of the city gate.

"Not like that. Take a puff. Then breathe in."

The hand in the mirror is slapping the face. The face grimaces and shows teeth; the eyes squint and close practically into half-moons; the mouth is grinning . . .

while a stone bounces off the teeth. The sharp end of a stick penetrates the eye, then pushes a hole in the flank, and stirs the abdomen violently until the stench overflows onto the stones of the river bed. A river of maggots is flowing through the carcass which is being hit by a stone and then another, and another. The stones sink into the decay and disappear into the movement of white worms. The stones are riddling the animal with a violence that sends blobs of decomposed matter spilling onto the bed.

She is guiding him into the hole and he is whirling the yellow tickle. But the aisle is empty. The man is trying to stand and walk while the soldiers are forcing him down. A car door slams, there is the sound of an engine, the grating of a gear, and the honking that will never recede around the corners of the city streets.

Fingers rub his cheeks. Fingers turn on the faucet. Worms reach for the soap, crawl over the soap, foam at the mouth, foam, crawl, wriggle, and rinse.

Over the hands and over the land. It has been raining for almost one week now: a long, continuous, steady downpour. The clouds have covered the mountains, have completely enveloped them, have rendered them invisible. Invisible also are the streams and rivulets running down the mountainside, down the ravines and the gorges—small tributaries feeding the river which emerges finally from under the curtain of clouds—emerges muddy, angry, roaring, and full of debris. The carcass of a horse rises and falls, appears and disappears, bobs up and down, is being swept downstream by the rough uneven tossing of the waves.

No, the horse is running away. The brown mare with

the white star in the middle of her forehead has bolted. She is racing toward the closed gate, pulling the empty milk cart behind her. The driver is running after her, waving a whip in the air, and yelling at her to stop. The animal is now galloping toward the iron gate. The wooden cart with the large wheels is bouncing over the dirt road. The distance between the gate is diminishing, has diminished, will have diminished completely the moment the mare hits the black grillework which has remained closed.

The horse is lying in the mud and the cart has overturned. A trickle of red is now staining the white star on the mare's forehead. The eyes are a dark brown, large, slightly bulged, and unmoving. An emaciated dog is sniffing a fresh, round, steaming globule of dung. People, voices, hands, and muddy boots are trying to make the horse get up. No one was there to open the gate. Those who witnessed the incident are saying that a fly bit her. Others are saying the dog scared her. Some think it was airplanes. Some contend that she went berserk. The men have unhitched the cart but the mare cannot get up.

The rain has swept away the retaining wall. Deep rivulets have eroded the stones and the pressure of the accumulated mud in the lupine bed has completely demolished the wall, strewing rocks haphazardly on the sloping ground below the garden.

A man is floating down the river while, on opposite banks, boys are hurling stones at each other. The man's son is afraid to jump into the river. Roger is diving into the muddy water. He is swimming toward the father. He is fighting the current, bobbing up and down, appearing and disappearing and, after what seems like an interminable struggle, reaches him, grabs him in a chest hold, and begins swimming back toward the shore.

The heat of the fire cannot be felt through the open door of the furnace. The flames are not dancing over a mass of coals framed by the square, nor are the flames consuming themselves endlessly as forked tongues. Perhaps.

The boy is reciting the Lord's Prayer. For the tenth time; and he now begins the first of ten Hail Marys. It is not cold outside yet he is wearing a heavy woolen sweater next to his skin. He is thinking that the sweater is perhaps not scratchy enough. He is walking along the pavement carefully avoiding the cracks. He must not step on any of the cracks in the pavement. He is retracing his steps as far as the church, even though he has just been there. He is re-entering the church now and kneeling to pray—saying once more the first of ten Lord's Prayers and ten Hail Marys. He is wishing the sweater were scratchier—counting the cracks in the pavement he will not step on—going back only as far as the church this time—not entering—but again carefully avoiding the cracks in the pavement. He derives satisfaction from the fact that he does not have to retrace his steps but that he is capable of doing so. Brother Polycarp would approve.

The robber, lashed tightly to the arms of the cross, is looking at the man nailed on the other cross beside him. He has a crown of thorns on His head and on His brow are the trickles of blood. "If Thou art the Son of God, I implore thee, forgive my transgressions." The Son of God opens His eyes, lifts His head slightly, and begins to move His lips. The lips are saying something, but the words are lost in the wind.

The same wind, no doubt, which is flapping the emblem of the cross—flapping it swiftly, snapping the seams briskly back and forth, rippling the red background and white circle of the cloth, whirling dozens of nebulae—thousands of crosses with broken arms that are now spreading the black pavement-scuffing runes.

The side-cars of the motorcycles bounce unevenly along the city streets and splash the puddles of rain water on the black boots of the men—the thousands of men who have set up camp in neat wooden barracks with red geraniums flowering in wooden windowsill planters. In spite of the geraniums the muzzles of the guns have etched themselves against the sky in long slanting diagonal lines—slanting along the same angle as the wind-driven rain, sleet, and snow.

The rain has matted the wool and run the red dye of the lambs. The tinkle of their bells is now muffled by the sound of the rain. Still they nibble the grass with a curling motion of their gray, almost black tongues, and the short jerky pull of the head and neck. The railroad cars moving north are full of tightly packed bleating sheep. The wheels make a clicking sound as the train accelerates, reduces the distance between the telephone poles and the up and down up and abrupt renewal of the flowing motion of the wires interrupted by the vertical presence of each pole flicking by in a continuous fluid intermingling of the blending and separating wire strands. The bodies lie in a smelly viscous mass. The bones are chilled by the trickle of water slanting into the cars through cracks in the boards.

Mara's yellow hair is, no doubt, chilled, matted, and stained now that the wind has blown all the stars out of the sky. The clouds of the storm are rolling sounds that split the heavens. On the hill overlooking the city are three crosses on which three men are barely visible in the sky's darkening violence. The only stars left are on men's lapels and on women's gray coats. But now that the stars are walking the streets they are never invisible.

The gun is aiming at the airplane and the sights are focusing on the center of the black cross. No. The gun is aiming at the big black cross painted on the side of a tank. No. It is aiming at the chest of a soldier walking down the street. The muzzle is hidden by the curtains of the window and it is pointing at the soldier's arm—pointing at the black swastika wrapped around his sleeve. The bullet is spinning the soldier around. He is falling to the pavement, reaching for his pistol and pointing it now at the second-story window. No. He is walking calmly down the street arm in arm with her. He has fallen to the pavement and she is bending over him, covering him with the black waves of her hair.

The patriarch slips on some loose stones but with unusual strength he retains his balance and the tablets are not broken.

"Thou shalt not kill!"

The muzzle of the gun is pointing at the insistent shadows between her legs. The chemise moves with the rhythm of her breathing and creases ever so slightly over the roundness of her breasts. Her black hair is frozen on the white surface of the pillow.

"Hell."

The magpie is lying motionless, its feathers ruffled,

while the wind drifts one feather to and fro in its interminable, oblique, and wavering descent to the ground.

He is reeling in the line, hand over hand, pulling the weight that is now rising and breaking the surface of the water. The scales, brown with occasional patches of gold, glint in the sunshine while the large tail wriggles over the jetty and thrashes itself still on the splintered boards of the dock. The gills are heaving wide now, showing tinges of rose on the inside while the mouth, with its two protruding appendages that look like whiskers, opens and closes, opens and closes.

It is not a heavy bird. The feet are black and shiny and as smooth as fish scales to the touch. A trickle of blood, some of which has stained his fingers, is running down the black beak. A trickle of red is also visible on the white star of the mare's forehead.

"Have you finished the poem?"

She is sewing crimson chrysanthemums in one corner of the handkerchief. The needle is moving rapidly, stitching the flowered design over the fine weave of the cloth. The thimble is pushing the needle and, each time it passes through the intermeshing fibers, the crimson thread blends into the pattern. The ray of sunshine, slanting diagonally into the room, illuminates the particles of dust, the tiny weightless filaments that are so distinctly visible in the light of the oblique ray. A current of air . . .

The wind swirls the autumn leaves, blows them in diagonal gusts of gold and red, rolls them pell-mell over the fields, and splashes the countryside with color. The trees are spilling over with yellow and crimson while wisps of

Mara's hair are being blown into the sky where the honking geese fly south. During the day the sun shines
brilliantly on the ice covering the pond while at night
the moon rushes through the clouds, through her lost fragrance, through lips and fingertips on which trickles of red
are visible. Something is spilling over the countryside, raining down from the heavens, and matting her golden hair.

"Your letters scare me sometimes and I wonder if it's
the you I know who has written them. I even feel guilty kissing you."

The trains are going north and the wheels are clicking
mile after mile along the tracks of steel that hold the ties
together, ties which are no longer visible as the parallel
converges to a pinpoint in the distance.

Two boys are running, balancing themselves on the
shiny, endless, elongated tracks, stepping occasionally on
a wooden tie, but running fast. One of them stumbles and
falls on the bed of sharp granite stones. There is a bad cut
on his knee and the blood is running down. Heavy railroad
spikes are embedded in the ties. The black square head
of the nail is holding his feet together. Blood is trickling
from the wound on his flank but the blood on his forehead
has now coagulated into storm clouds which are raining a
delayed violence. In the distance the ties along the tracks
of steel are not visible. Mara is in a car going north. The
flag is flapping in the wind, flapping the black wings of
its emblem against a sky full of speculation. The seasons
continue to rain petals of color from the trees while the
wind blows them in long diagonal thrusts of yellow and
red.

"I love you so much. Love is such a spiritual thing that

I could never sully it." Our love is as pure as the flight of two birds circling the moon, as ethereal as the winged contact of their feathered glide that breathes with the union of uplifted selves winging our oneness toward the eternal circle.

But the reflections of the sun on the ice pond hurt the eyes and grind into the retinas with sharp daggers of light. The wind makes the eyes run with tears. It is the same wind that has etched the sky with flaming wings. The sun is whirling dozens of nebulae into circles of white. Black crosses are now orbiting the sky and hurtling through space, backward, toward the womb of time.

Golden daggers are still scaling the eyes, blinding the retinas with bird tracks that split into ellipses of white and black. The soul is burning in a red immobility that clutches the throat and stifles the cry.

"You must have fallen asleep."

She is stroking his head, gently, back and forth, with her hand—talking to him, soothing the fever of his brow, tucking the sheets and blanket under his chin, stroking his forehead and his hair, asking him if he was dreaming, commenting on his fretfulness, begging him to answer her, his own mother, searching his eyes for some sign, sitting down again in the chair next to the bed, in the chair where she has been sewing, where she is now sewing again, where the needle is moving through the white fabric of the cloth, where it will no doubt continue to weave its pattern. The crimson chrysanthemums are almost finished now. The needle is weaving the in-and-out design of the last flower while the ray of sunshine is slanting diagonally through the closed window.

The ray is illuminating the particles of dust. The lower diagonal is absolutely parallel to the upper one and it is only within this narrow band of light, no wider perhaps than six inches, that the weightless filaments are visible.

Sunlight is illuminating the corner of the room where the two walls meet. The needle, however, is still moving through the weave of the handkerchief, stitching the design of white on the white background of the cloth. Each time it passes through the intermeshing fibers, the thread blends into the pattern.

She needs a new thread now. She is holding the needle at eye level—holding it up to the window so the light will pass through the tiny opening, moistening the white strand between her lips and tongue and trying to insert the tip. The strand is going through now, barely, even though the thread is of the thinnest imaginable. She is pulling the two strands together and tying a knot on one end with a deft maneuver of her right hand and fingers. She is inserting the needle into the cloth. The needle is weaving a design that will again take place in any one of the four corners.

The snow has been falling for days now, falling through the air, covering the roads and fields with high drifts, covering the checkered fields with white, a covering interrupted, here and there, by a diagonal road or the apparently aimless meandering of a river which loops around itself before it disappears. The thimble is pushing the needle through the cloth while, on the other side, nimble fingers retrieve it, reinsert the tip and, with an apparently endless continuity, repeat the necessary motions for the elaboration of the pattern—a pattern illuminated by whatever light is passing through the eye . . .

. . . of the needle.